Calley's Cottage

to Carrie,

April 2006

Calley's Cottage

a beautiful young lady —

Fondly, Bettye Grogan

Bettye D. Grogan

Pleasant W rd

ISBN 1-4141-0561-4
Library of Congress Catalog Card Number: 2005907967

Dedication

To my family,
With love

Acknowledgments

Gratitude goes to my colleagues at Hoptown Writers who listen to and critique my work weekly. A special thanks to Terri Parker for her editing skills and for the hours she spent on this book.

I am blessed with family and friends in many places who urge me to keep on writing with your kind words and encouragement. There are too many to name; you know who you are. I thank God for you every day. Without you this book would have never been written.

Chapter 1

Calley's Cottage

Twilight crept into the corners of the room, banishing the red ball that had filled the large bedroom with a fiery glow at sunset. Ginny Lee first noticed the silence of the birds before she opened her eyes and realized that the light was dimming. She had not been asleep, merely resting her tired eyes. There would be little sleep in the hours ahead: too many conflicting thoughts whirled in her brain, too many painful emotions tugged at her heart.

Somehow the deepening shadows offered little comfort as they settled around the old house, bringing back memories of the younger Ginny slipping up to this feminine wonderland of silk and softness. She used to do her best thinking here in her grandmother's bedroom, propped up among the down pillows, left alone to daydream. But her grandmother—the lovely woman who had bequeathed her this house—had deceived her.

"How could you, Grammy?" she murmured as she sat up, pushing the mass of pillows behind her angrily and frowning at her surroundings. The faded cabbage rose wallpaper in muted tones of green and pink wrapped the room in pale beauty. Her hand gently drifted over the handmade crocheted spread that hung gracefully over a pink silk skirt, faded from years of sun. The antique dresser and the tall headboard and footboard were walnut, darkened with even more time. They had been her great-grandmother's furnishings. Small paintings of landscapes hung on each side of the dresser and a large seascape was over the small settee between the two large windows. What had always been a dreamy refuge suddenly seemed like a stark nightmare that had descended upon her.

The evening breeze, lightly swaying the ruffles of the organdy curtains, brought a chill to replace the warmth of the spring afternoon. She rose and closed the window with a bang, turning again to the old roll-top desk. Sliding back into the chair, she looked at the papers that she had scattered earlier before throwing herself across the bed in frustration and disbelief. She wished that she had never found that bundle of letters inside the old paid bill file, never removed the yarn binding and read them. Some were love letters to her grandmother from her grandfather, sweet, romantic, precious letters that she bundled back up to be saved and laid them aside.

She picked up one of the other letters. They were in the formal stylized handwriting of her grandmother and were addressed to her mother. She had wondered at first why they would be mixed in with her grandmother's love letters, and curiosity made her open them. Now she wished she had bundled them up, unread, with the letters from her grandfather and put them in her grandmother's trunk.

Her eyes filled with tears as she remembered that Laura Belle Cantrell, so much a loving influence in her life, had been gone for only a month. So many times since her arrival this morning, Ginny Lee had expected to see her come through a door or call out from another room. But the silence was only broken by Grace Capshaw, a neighbor and dear friend, as she came and went with food and comfort during the day.

Turning on the desk lamp, she blinked away the tears and began to read again from the yellowed, wrinkled letter in her hand. It was to her mother, Alison Cantrell, when she was young and in college.

Darling,
You don't know how hard it was to leave you yesterday. If your father had not been so ill, I would never have left you, would have rented a house so you could be with me and not have to deal with this alone. I hope that the search for John will end soon, and we can see him brought to trial for what he did to you. Even though the police said there was not enough evidence, I feel sure that if he came back, we could find a way to make him admit his guilt. You said he would never be found, but his family will have to tell us where he is eventually. Things will work out, you'll see. But now just keep telling yourself that it was NOT your fault. You had no idea he was that kind of person.

Her eyes slid down the page, skipping over the assurances of love and support that her grandmother wrote to her mother. Placing it face down, she went to the other letters and put them in order by the dates in the left corner. Carrying them to the bed, she switched on the bedside light, flung herself against the pillows and read the next letter, focusing on the third paragraph.

Alison, you must go to the doctor immediately. Come home next week, and I'll make you an appointment with Dr. Crane. You've known him all your life, and you won't be so afraid. I can't mention this on the phone for fear your father might overhear us. He's a little suspicious of my two trips to see you. Please call and let me know if you're coming so I can talk to Dr. Crane.

Hurriedly she scanned the rest and picked up the third letter. Her hand trembled as she held the paper closer to her eyes and swallowed down the lump in her throat as she read.

Why did you go back to school without saying goodbye to your father and me? Dr. Crane called after you left his office, and I waited for you to come home all day. I know you are upset, Alison, but you aren't the first young woman to become pregnant because of rape. It's a hard thing to deal with, but there is a baby to consider. You know you must not get yourself into such a state that you would destroy that living being inside you. Please come home. We can raise the child together. Your father doesn't have long to live; you realize that, don't you? I know this is a double tragedy for us both, but he doesn't have to know. He will be gone before the child is born, and we will need each other then. You can finish school later. I'm enclosing money for your ticket. Please don't stay there and mope and worry.

She dropped the paper with a sigh and turned her head to the picture of her mother on the table. Picking up the heavy gilded frame, her finger traced the outline of her mother's image–lovely dark hair, brown eyes, a smile that showed perfect teeth—a typical pose for a graduation picture. Her mother, Alison, looked so much like her grandmother, Laura Belle. The picture could have been Laura Belle with another hairstyle, in another time.

She rose and walked slowly to the dresser. Tilting the mirror a little to better see herself, she surveyed her own image. A cascade of auburn hair curled wildly around her slightly square face dusted with a sprinkling of freckles across the straight narrow nose. She had the pale skin of a redhead and green eyes that slanted slightly upward.

Thinking back, she remembered asking her mother, "My hair isn't black like yours and Grammy's. Who do I look like, Mommy?" Her mother had hugged her close. "You look like your father, Honey." Then, "How did my father die, Mommy?" Her mother had frowned as she put her down and began to turn down the bed. "I've told you, Ginny Lee. He died in a bad car wreck." She clearly recalled kneeling beside her bed to pray for the kind gentle man who had been her father, the man who would be putting her to bed if he were only there.

Ginny pinched the bridge of her nose as she remembered that later, when she was older, her mother had explained that he had been cremated and his ashes scattered over the mountains. Since Alison said she wanted to keep her maiden name, Ginny never questioned why her name wasn't the same as her father's. His name, John Fredericks, was seldom mentioned. Alison and Laura Belle had told her that there were no other grandparents living. As time passed, she asked fewer questions. When her schoolmates asked where her daddy was, she told them about the wreck, and they felt sorry for her. But growing up in a household of two women was tempered with cousins and friends, and her great uncle Joe had been a father figure until his recent death. Ginny had not felt deprived as she got older; this was the only life she knew.

Her mother and grandmother were women of faith. Ginny's whole life revolved around church activities and community responsibilities; it was just a way of life in the Cantrell family. How could the two of them have lived this lie for all these years while teaching Ginny to respect the truth?

She looked back in the mirror, feeling hurt and angry at her own reflection. Yes, she probably did look like her father. But he wasn't the kindly, loving man she had imagined. He was a rapist. Her mother and grandmother had lied. She could never face her beloved grandmother again to ask her why. But she could—and would–face her mother. Alison was coming home tomorrow, and they were going to spend the next few days cleaning out Laura Belle's things and putting the house up for sale. She would get some answers from her mother, and this time she would find out the truth.

Chapter 2

Alison pulled her small car up the driveway and turned off the engine. She sat for a moment, looking over the old pale green Victorian house, the house she had lived in for most of her life. Four years ago, Ginny's first year in college, she had moved to Louisville and accepted a job there. But the old house was still home to her.

It was still a beautiful place with Laura Belle's tulips and hyacinths blooming around the steps. But the hedges needed trimming badly, and the magenta paint trim on the front windows was peeling. Obviously, there was more to be repaired than she had noticed during her mother's brief illness and death. Pangs of sorrow washed over her; sorrow and regret that she had not spent more time here in this lovely home with her wonderful mother before the cancer struck with such ferocity.

She had been excited about spending a whole week with her daughter, even if it did include a lot of hard work getting the house in shape. Going through her mother's things would be emotionally difficult, but with Ginny there, it would be easier. And with Ginny in her first year of teaching, they had such little time together, even though they only lived fifty miles apart.

Shaking off the memory of her loss, Alison pushed up her sweater sleeve and looked at her watch. Nine o'clock. She had made good time. They could have a cup of coffee and catch up before they knuckled down to work.

Pulling open the hatchback, she wrestled her heavy suitcase to the ground, leaving a box of assorted groceries and cleaning supplies to be dealt with later. She pulled her bag behind her up the steps onto the wide porch with its swing swaying slightly in the breeze. "The porch needs painting, too," she murmured to herself, glancing around as she fingered her key chain for the house key to open the heavy leaded glass door.

The front hall felt chilly, and a fine layer of dust lay over the library table and the grandfather's clock. "Hmmm, will a week be long enough to get everything done?" she wondered aloud. Slipping off her shoulder bag onto the hall tree, she followed the smell of coffee that wafted on the air.

"Ginny? Where are you, honey?" Moving through the dining room around its mahogany furniture into the kitchen, she found her daughter at the small table, her hands wrapped around her coffee cup.

"Hello, sweetheart. It's so good to see you." Alison reached for Ginny who half rose to accept her hug. "Oh, thank you for having a pot of coffee made. I left without a thing but a bottle of water." She picked up the cup Ginny had left by the stove and poured it full, then doctored it with sweetener and creamer. Taking a sip, she pronounced it the best she'd ever tasted.

As she sat down across from Ginny, she noticed how quiet her daughter was. There were circles under her green eyes and her face was a little flushed. A small alarm went off as it always did when she suspected her daughter might be ill.

"Honey, are you sick? You don't look so good. And you're still in your robe. What gives?"

"I'm fine, Mom," Ginny said softly. She cleared her throat and spoke louder. "You're looking great. How's the job going?"

"Wonderful. I have to pinch myself when I think how lucky I am to get this job with no more experience than I have. Thank goodness for Cousin Charles. He's a wonderful boss, and not just to me, but to everyone in the office. But I'm always telling you that, aren't I?" She paused, waiting for a comment, then went on. "So you got here yesterday? Did you have any trouble sleeping in this creaky old house with no one else here?"

"I didn't sleep very well." Ginny admitted softly. "I'd forgotten how loud that clock in the hall is. I don't remember hearing it all the way upstairs before."

"Well, there were usually other people in the house and you didn't notice. Oh, I stopped and picked up some donuts for our coffee break. They're in the car. I'll be right back."

Ginny watched her jump up and hurry out the kitchen door. "She looks so young," she thought as she listened to the click of her mother's heels on the wooden floors. "No one could have been a better mother, and I do love her so much. I wish we didn't have to have this talk. I wish I hadn't found those letters. We'd be laughing and working together without these bad feelings hovering over us." Her anger had cooled somewhat, and a strange sense of guilt had gathered around her heart; guilt for having to hurt her mother to get at the truth. She wondered for a moment if she should just forget the letters. But she knew it would weigh heavily on her if she didn't get things out in the open. There could be no way to get around this confrontation.

Alison returned, set the box on the counter, and ripped open the package, all the while complaining about the ten pounds she had gained the past year. Popping the donuts in the toaster oven to warm them, she reached into the cabinet and placed two dessert plates on the table, casting a side-glance at her daughter. "You're awfully quiet, sweetie. Is something wrong?"

"Mom…I found these," Ginny began shakily, then pulled the letters from her robe pocket and slid them across the table.

Alison wiped her hands on a towel as she reached for the papers. "What's this, some old love notes?" She glanced at the first page, and her face froze as she recognized Laura Belle's writing. "Where did you find these?" Her voice was shaking almost as much as her hands as she glanced through the pages. Her heart pounded; dread and anxiety flooded her body. Her knees felt as though they could no longer support her weight.

"I was looking through the desk upstairs. There was a package of old pictures taken at one of my birthday parties. Grammy's letters from Grandpa were right under them, and these letters were in the middle of the bundle.

"Why did she save them? If you didn't want me to know the truth, why weren't they thrown away? I wish they had been. Never in my wildest dreams would I believe that my mother and grandmother had lied to me all my life, deliberately lied. It makes me so angry…" her voice rose and she slapped the table with her hands.

Alison jumped at the sound. Avoiding her daughter's eyes, she sighed and laid the papers on the table. As she rose and reached for the coffee pot and refilled their cups, she tried to calm the whirling thoughts in her brain. There were questions from Ginny that would have to be answered now that the family secret had been discovered. She reached for Ginny's hand, but Ginny defiantly slid both hands under the table.

Alison took a deep breath and began. "Ginny, I gave mother's letters back to her. Actually, I threw them at her. I came home from college, and we had an awful fight. I had no idea that she saved them or why she did. Maybe she didn't really mean to; maybe they just got in with the other letters she saved."

"You didn't want to have me, did you? I can see why you wouldn't. A child of rape; what a disgrace! You should have given me up for adoption and avoided this whole mess." Ginny's voice trembled with fresh fury.

Putting her hand to her heart, as if that would stop the ache, Alison protested loudly. "No, honey, no. I was scared to death, I admit. But I didn't want to get rid of you; that was against my beliefs. I would never, NEVER have put you up for adoption. As you grew in me, I began to love you very much. You were MY baby.

"Back to the quarrel between Mother and me. She wanted me to stay here and have you, and I wanted to go up to Aunt Edna's, away from everyone. I didn't want to face my friends. But Mother put her foot down."

"So that's when you made up all the lies? God forgive you! God forgive you both!"

Alison flinched. "Yes. We made it all up. Back in those days you did that to save face. And I prayed for forgiveness every night for living that lie. Later, your grandmother begged me to tell you the truth, and I agreed. But then she became so ill, and I put those thoughts aside. We wanted to protect you."

"Mom! That was the eighties, for goodness sake. You talk like it was a hundred years ago."

"I know, but your grandmother was very old-fashioned about things, as you well know. And this was a small town. Oh, Ginny, I hoped you'd never find out any of this. We made up the story so you'd feel secure and loved."

"Who else knows?" Ginny pulled the curtain open and watched a redbird in the shrub as the tears seeped into the corners of her eyes.

"Only Dr. Crane and Grace. Both were such good friends with your grandmother."

"Grace knew? And she never told anyone? That's hard to believe."

"Grace loved us all like family, you know that. She would never give it away, for all our sakes."

Ginny sighed and dropped the curtain. "Of course not. There aren't many friends like her. Well, since I know my origins, I'd like you to tell me about it. I think I have the right to know the whole story now. The truth, Mom—no more lies. No more protecting me. I want to know exactly what happened with my father."

Alison rubbed her forehead, trying to wipe away the headache that had suddenly begun to throb behind her eyes. The whole truth. That would require delving back into old memories, old hurts.

"Yes, you do deserve to hear all about it," she said softly. Let's go into the living room. I'll tell you what happened. But first, I want you to know that in spite of the lies we told you, your grandmother and I did it because we loved you with all our hearts. You were the center of our lives. You know that, don't you?" She stood and pulled Ginny into her arms. Ginny breathed a loud sigh and laid her head on her mother's shoulder.

Alison held her until she pulled back, brushed her damp bangs out of her eyes, and walked ahead of her mother into the cheery living room, collapsing on the red brocade sofa. In the past, when they had weighty matters to discuss, Ginny had put her head in her mother's lap as they talked. But when Alison patted her lap, Ginny turned away and curled into the corner of the sofa. Alison sighed and reached for a pillow to clutch to her chest, tucked her legs beneath her, and began her story.

Chapter 3

1979

I was in the cafeteria trying to study for a psychology test while I ate a quick breakfast. My mind kept wandering to the window and the quad beyond. It was a beautiful day, sunny and warm, and I couldn't keep my thoughts on the page. Then I remembered how much I needed a good grade in that class and got up to go to the library where it was quiet. I bumped into my friend, Paul, as I turned the corner.

"Hey, little buddy. Where you headed in such a rush?"

"Hi, Paul. What are you up to?"

"I'm thinking about taking a long walk around the reservoir. It's too pretty a day to waste inside. Want to come along?" Paul was pulling me toward the door and grinning. It didn't take me long to agree. The sunshine beckoned, and psychology lost the battle.

"Great idea. Pick me up in front of the dorm?"

"Ten minutes?"

"Make it fifteen."

I hurried over to the dorm and changed into my old jeans and a flannel shirt, slathered on lip gloss, and grabbed two soft drinks from my refrigerator. Paul was just driving up when I ran down the steps.

Paul and I were best friends, buddies from the very first day of school. We consoled each other when potential romances went awry, and made good dates for each other when there were no special dates available. He was like the brother I never had. I trusted him completely.

When I reached the car, a tall auburn haired young man stepped out and held the door for me. I'd seen him around campus, sometimes with Paul, and I knew that his name was John Fredericks.

"You remember John, don't you?" Paul asked, leaning across from the driver's seat. "I ran into him going to my car. He felt like he could use some fresh air, too."

"Great. How ya doin', John?"

He smiled at me. He had such beautiful white teeth, even and straight. Anyway, I got into the front seat with Paul, and we took off. I gave my friend a questioning look, but he shrugged in innocence. Paul drove an ancient Volkswagen, and it ambled through the narrow streets and up Ninth Street hill, coughing and sputtering up the steep climb to the reservoir. Once there, we parked and walked to the lake, sparkling and clear in the morning sun. I still remember how clear that lake was then.

"It's so pretty up here, so peaceful." I found a log and sat down in the warm sun. "Makes you forget about schedules and classes and papers, doesn't it?"

"I wish I could forget. I've got English at three, and a book review that I should be writing." John rolled his eyes. They were the color of the ocean when it was stormy, a soft grey-green. I couldn't help staring at his beautiful eyes. Then I covered up my embarrassment with a lame answer about how he shouldn't be there at all, should be back at the library, studying.

"I'll take hiking over studying anytime. I'll go on to class and make up some excuse. My grades are good, so it won't cost me a lot. Besides, I've been bugging Paul to introduce me to you for weeks. He's so protective–I'll swear he's like your body guard."

"I have to approve of the people my little buddy associates with," Paul said in his defense.

"Well, we'd better move if we're going to get John back at three." I pulled away and moved out in front. We hiked the rim of the lake, stopping to skip rocks, to push and threaten each other with a dunking in the cold water. The conversation turned to our families. I found out that John was an only child, like me, and that his parents were recently divorced and very angry with each other.

When they let me out at the dorm at two forty-five, I had a date with John for the next night, and I could hardly wait.

Paul called later. "Little buddy, be careful. I probably wouldn't have introduced him to you if he hadn't bugged me for so long. I think he's an ok guy, but he's a little cocky. Just watch it, all right?"

"Don't worry, Paul. I can take care of myself. And thanks for bringing him today. I think he's really cute. He seems very nice to me."

Our first date was dinner at the Roundtree, the local hangout back then. We ate hamburgers and played pool. I had never played before, but he was very patient. Walking back to the dorm on a moonlit night was very romantic. We sat outside the dorm and talked until I just had to go in.

I waited for him to call, but it was two long weeks before he asked me out again. I had planned to say no, to play a little hard to get. But when he suggested that we drive out of town to dinner at a lodge in the hills, I couldn't resist. After trying on almost everything in my wardrobe, I settled on a bright yellow pantsuit I thought looked good with my dark hair. Then I spent another hour with a curling iron, trying to get it to look just right.

"Wow!" he exclaimed as I got into his car. "You look beautiful."

Flustered, I blushed and changed the subject. "I love your car." Not many of us had new cars back then, and I was very impressed with his lovely new Buick.

"Thanks. My dad bought this for me last year. I think it's supposed to take the sting out of their divorce—and keep me in school."

"You wouldn't drop out this late in the game, would you?" I asked as we drove away from the dorm.

"I thought about it last year. Things were so bad at home. I was so bogged down and didn't know what I wanted to do. But I decided this year that being an engineer like Dad won't be such a bad deal after all. He makes good money, has plenty of time off. Of course, that may be what got him in trouble, I don't know.

Anyway, I'm hanging in there. And I'm getting through most of my classes without too much difficulty."

"I could never get through some of those courses—too hard."

"Teaching school sounds easier, huh?"

"To me, it does."

The drive in the hills at sunset was so lovely that we stopped at a pullover to look at the view. It was the prettiest sunset I'd ever seen, all those gorgeous shades of purple, pink, and peach layered across the sky. He held my hand as we stood there, and my heart skipped a beat.

The old stone lodge was set back in the woods. In the dining room, little lantern lights at each table gave a magical glow to the wood paneled room. Our dinner was delicious—potato soup, chicken with roasted vegetables and lemon pie. I remember that clearly because it was the best food I'd ever had in such a long time, except for your grandmother's cooking, of course. We lingered over coffee until the dining room cleared out, and we knew we had to leave.

At the door of the dorm, he kissed me, a sweet tender kiss that I wanted to go on and on. But he let me go with a light kiss on the nose. I watched him walk away and turn to give me a wave. Then I took the elevator up to my third floor room, unlocked my door, and collapsed onto the bed in a fit of delirious laughter.

I was madly in love after only two dates.

Chapter 4

After that, we saw each other as often as possible, eating lunch together two days a week and studying at the library between classes. We were both busy with different pursuits, but we managed to squeeze in dates whenever we could. I went home every other weekend, but John usually stayed on campus because of his rocky relationship with his parents.

Just before Christmas break, an unexpected snow blanketed the area. Even classes were called off (a rare occurrence), and we scholars were out in force, playing in the snow. A few were out on cross-country skis, but the largest number was on Ninth Street hill with sleds.

We joined the group on the hill, commandeered a friend's sled, and took several rides down the hill. Laughing like crazy, we took turns pulling each other back up the slope until our legs ached from the exertions. Snowball fights broke out, and we ended up on opposite sides, pelting each other until our coats were white and wet.

As darkness set in and temperatures dropped into the teens, the bonfire wasn't enough to warm cold hands and toes, so the party began to break up for food and coffee at the local fast food places.

"I have an idea," John said as we were wringing out our wet gloves. "Let's pick up some food and go over to my friend Matt's place. He's got a fireplace."

"Where is Matt? Won't he care if we just barge into his apartment without asking?"

"He's home; his mother had surgery today. And no, he won't care. He told me to use it whenever I wanted."

Something told me that might not be a good idea, but the thought of food and a warm fireplace overrode my instincts. So we picked up hot sandwiches and coffee and walked to Matt's apartment behind the local hangout. It was in an old, but well kept house, and the rooms were roomy and neat, though chilly.

Keeping on our coats, we turned the oven on low to keep the sandwiches warm while we struggled to get a fire going. Since John failed to open the damper, the apartment quickly filled with smoke. Coughing and fanning the air, we finally opened the painted over windows, and the frigid air cleared out the worst of the smoke. John found some drier wood on the porch, and we eventually had a roaring fire. We ate sitting on the floor in front of it, letting the heat warm our frozen hands and feet. Only when the fire got too hot did we move back to the sofa.

"This was the nicest day," I said with a contented sigh.

"Yes, it was," he agreed. He pulled me over to him, and we covered up with a quilt that smelled like pizza and assorted fast food. The warmth of the fire after the strenuous afternoon's exercise soon put us both to sleep.

When I woke up I felt his lips on my neck. I stretched and pulled away from him. Then I laughed at his face, all wrinkled where he slept on the folds of the quilt.

"How long have we slept?"

"Too long," he answered. Pulling me back into his arms, he kissed me. I felt myself liking it too much and struggled to pull away.

"Whoa," I said, sitting up. "It's been a long day. Maybe you'd better take me back to the dorm."

"Why? You know that we're starting to have strong feelings for each other. Can't you just relax and let go?"

"I do care about you, John, but I don't want this to go too far. That's not how I operate." I threw the quilt aside and started to get up.

"I'm sorry. I didn't mean to pressure you into anything. It just felt so good to be close to you here all wrapped up in this quilt. Stay awhile. I'll behave, I promise." He wrinkled his nose and gave me that wide brilliant smile, and my heart melted. So I stayed. I knew that things were going too fast, but I didn't know that he wouldn't stop. And he had promised.

When he relaxed his hold on me, I sprang up, grabbing my coat, and ran out of the house, bursting into frantic tears as I ran. I stumbled across yards and through alleys all the way back to the dorm. He followed in the car as closely as he could, stopping periodically to call out to me in desperation, trying to get me into the car. I screamed "no" at him until I reached the walkway to the dorm, and I had to stop and catch my breath.

The erratic pounding of my heart frightened me, I was sure I was going to have an attack. Sweat was pouring down my face, yet I was shivering violently. I wanted to lie down in the cold snow and curl up into a ball, I was so tired. But he had gotten out of the car and was running toward me.

"Please, Alison. Wait. Let me apologize. I didn't intend to...Oh, please wait..."

"Get away from me!" I forced my feet to move down the slippery sidewalk and hurled myself through the door of the dorm. Two girls were pulling on boots in the lobby, so I pretended to blow my nose as I passed, covering up my face with the tissue to avoid their stares. Thankfully the elevator was empty, and my heart began to slow down as I reached my room.

I slammed the door and slid down to the floor. In a few minutes the phone began to ring. I lay on the cold tile with my eyes closed, ignoring it. My mind felt ready to explode. How could I be so dumb as to trust John? He had never been like that before. Why didn't he take 'no' for an answer? I had loved him, I really did. He hurt me, not just physically, but emotionally. He broke my heart.

Finally throwing off my wet coat, I grabbed my robe and towel and went to the showers. I turned the water on hot and stood under it until my skin was red and shriveled, and I felt warmth creeping into my bones. But when I climbed into the bed, there was no sleep, even though I had taken the phone off the hook and the dorm was unusually quiet. The shameful scene flashed through my mind as the hours crept by. Every time I dropped off to sleep, I would wake up in tears.

In a daze the next day, I stumbled through the exam. When the agony of the test was over, I left the classroom and went back to the dorm, picked up my bag that I had packed that morning, and took a cab to the bus station.

The ride home seemed like an eternity. The old man sitting next to me kept slipping over on my shoulder in a drunken stupor. I pushed him over again and again, feeling nauseous at the smell of the liquor on his breath. Finally the bus pulled into town, and I gratefully grabbed my bag as it was unloaded and took off on foot. Walking the six blocks to the house, I had to pause a few times to set the bag down and rest.

When I turned down our street and saw my home, I almost cried. I'd never been so glad to see the old house in my life. The sun was setting, and the glow reflected from the glass, almost like candles in the windows. I fumbled in my purse for my key, and not finding it, I began to bang on the door in frustration.

"Alison!" Laura Belle exclaimed as she threw open the door. "Come in, darling. Did you lose your key?" She threw her arms around me, taking the bag out of my hands. "We didn't expect you until tomorrow. Why on earth didn't you call; we'd have picked you up. I can't believe you walked all the way from the…"

"Mom, it's so good to be home." I blinked back tears as I pulled off my coat, hung it on the hall tree, and squeezed my mother's hands. I was so very grateful to be home where I could block out the scene with John, if only for awhile. Laura Belle pulled me toward the stairs and called out, "Bill? Bill, come down. Our daughter is home for Christmas."

Chapter 5

The house was quiet except for the musical chimes of the grandfather clock as it struck ten. Sunlight shone through the lace curtains making intricate patterns on the wooden floor. Allison had finished telling Ginny the details of her relationship with her father, and the silence was heavy with unspoken words.

Ginny sat facing her mother, her head resting against the old high back sofa. She ran her fingers over the brocade pattern, tracing the design, quietly reflecting on the pain heard in her mother's voice as she told the story. Finally, she reached over and touched her mother's shoulder. Alison responded with a tentative smile.

"I know you must have questions, honey. Ask me anything; now is the time to get it all out in the open."

Ginny looked down at her hands as she picked at a hangnail. "Poor Mom," she said softly. "You must have been devastated."

"I was. I found out that I was pregnant when I went back to school after Christmas break. You know the rest from the letters. I left school and your grandmother made up the story about the bogus marriage and accident that left me a widow."

"It's hard to believe that anyone believed that twenty something years ago. It sounds so phony."

"Not everyone did believe our story, I'm sure, but it made your grandmother feel better. Your grandfather died months before you were born. That was a shock to everyone, the whole town, in fact. Not many knew how sick he was. Everyone was so kind and sympathetic. If my situation was ever questioned, I never knew about it."

"What happened to John? Did you bring charges?"

"No."

"Why not, Mom?"

"It would mean that everyone here would find out. Things like that don't stay secret."

"Well, what did he have to say to you when you confronted him? It must have been so painful to face him again."

"John left school at Christmas break. My friend, Paul, talked to both his parents to try and locate him. He didn't tell them why he was so anxious to find him. John's mother said he called her from Kansas, and said he was on his way to California. His father hadn't heard a word—or so he said. John never knew of my pregnancy, Ginny."

"Your friend, Paul, knew all about it?" Ginny moved closer to her mother.

"Yes. He asked me to marry him to give my baby a name, but I said "no". He felt like it was his fault since he introduced John to me, which, of course, was silly. But he remained a good friend through it all until he married and moved to Canada."

After a long pause, Ginny sighed and reached for her mother's hand. "Did you ever find out where John ended up?"

"No. After you came, we were so beguiled with you. As you grew, it no longer seemed important that he be found. And, by that time, the story had become part of our lives. I think we almost believed it ourselves."

Ginny's mind went back to the years that she thought her mother a widow—a woman who never went out with another man, a mother who worked at a low paying job at the school so she could have the same hours as her child. Yet, she never smothered her daughter. Ginny had always been trusted to follow her own judgment.

"You never dated, Mom."

"No. You and Laura Belle filled my life." Alison felt her emotions give way, and tears began to flow down her cheeks.

"What you must have gone through all those years." Ginny moved to Alison's side and threw her arms around her. Her fierce anger at being deceived melted into her mother's tears.

After a few minutes, Alison wiped her eyes. "Can you forgive me?"

"There's nothing to forgive. I love you, Mom. I just wish you'd told me the truth long ago."

"I wish I had, too. You know, the funny thing about living a lie is that you come to believe it yourself. At first I felt guilty about keeping you away from your other grandparents. But when you were small, I heard through Paul that John's mother died from cancer, and his dad was killed in an accident shortly after. Theirs was such a tragic family." Alison grimaced as she rose, stomping a foot that had gone to sleep. "I'm going to get some aspirin, honey. My head is splitting."

"Why don't we forget about the clean up today, Mom?"

"No, sweetie. I'll be fine in a bit. We need to get our hands busy. We can talk as we work. I feel like if we don't get started now, I won't want to do anything all weekend."

So they began sorting through closets and drawers, sifting through Laura Belle's things, pausing to cry a little, laugh a little. They worked through lunch since neither was hungry. When late afternoon came, Grace stepped across the yard carrying her picnic basket. She opened the back door, calling in her tremulous voice, "Hello?"

"In the back bedroom, Grace."

Pausing in the kitchen to deposit her basket, Grace pushed a wispy strand back into the tortoiseshell clip holding her long gray hair, and greeted her friends in the back hall. A tiny woman, she had to reach up to deliver hugs to Alison and Ginny.

"You darling," Alison said, pulling away from her embrace. "I smell fried chicken, smelled it when you came in the door. What else did you bring us?" Grace grinned and beckoned, and they followed her to the kitchen. Throwing back the top of the basket, she proudly displayed chicken, potato salad, baked beans, and chess pie.

"I adore you, Grace," Ginny sighed happily. Taking tea from the refrigerator, they heaped their plates high and started for the dining room.

"No," said Grace. "Let's eat on the back porch. It's warmer out than it was earlier, and I want you to see the tulips and that big dogwood. Spectacular!"

They settled into the worn wicker chairs and surveyed the beauty. "It is spectacular," Alison agreed. The bed of tulips was a riot of every color, and the dogwood was just coming into full bloom. "Did you plant those tulips? I don't think Mother was able to do much of anything last fall."

"I added a few to the ones she put out the year before. I had some left over that I didn't have a place for."

After awhile, Grace got up to get the pie and some dessert plates. Looking at Ginnys' plate, she stopped. "You haven't eaten very much, Missy. Wasn't your chicken good?"

"It was delicious, Grace. I'm just not as hungry as I thought I was."

"Sit down, Grace. We need to tell you something." Alison grabbed the tiny hand and motioned her back into her chair.

"What's going on…," Grace's weathered face drew up in a frown as she read the solemn look in Alison's eyes.

"Grace, Ginny knows about her father."

"Oh, dear. How did this come about?" Grace looked at Ginny's averted face.

"Ginny found some old letters that my mother wrote me, and she begged me to tell her the whole story. She knows about the lies, but I hope, by now, she is beginning to understand why we did what we did." Alison looked hopefully at Ginny. There was silence for a moment.

Then Ginny answered. "I'm trying to understand, I really am. Grace, I feel so badly about what happened to Mom. I know she went through a great deal, and I'm grateful that she had me and all that. But that ruse was so silly, and in the end it hurt me more. How could you go along with it? You're the dearest friend we have in the whole world."

"Laura Belle was like a sister to me. I loved her very much. If she thought the story about your father was the best way to handle the situation, then I wasn't going to give it away. They never thought you'd find out, Ginny. They would have never hurt you, you know that." She sat down by Ginny on the settee and put her arms around her.

Ginny lowered her head to the slender shoulder. "I know, I know. But I thought my life was so perfect, except for having a dead father. I even thought I looked like him, since I don't look like Mom."

"You do look like him," Alison said softly.

"You know, I really don't feel like talking about this any more today," Ginny said, rising. "If you two don't mind, I think I'll go up to Grammy's room. I'm pretty worn out. It's been a long day."

Alison kissed her daughter's cheek. "Get a good hot bath, honey. We'll see you in the morning."

Ginny paused in the doorway. "Thanks for the supper, Grace. You've always been my second grandmother, and now you're my first. You know I love you, don't you?"

Grace nodded, and tears welled up in her blue eyes as she watched the young woman, whom she had loved from a baby, turn away with a tremendous burden on her heart.

Chapter 6

Together, they got through the week, cleaning out closets and drawers and dividing up prized mementos. Ginny asked questions, Alison answered. Toward the end of the week, Ginny seemed resigned to the answers her mother gave her and settled into surface acceptance. But nights, in Laura Belle's bed, visions haunted her, visions of her mother suffering an unwanted pregnancy and the father who gave her red hair and green eyes.

The last night before having to return to their jobs, they took Grace out to dinner. She had been a blessing, as always, to help them pack up Laura Belle's things and to provide sandwiches and soup during the week. They ate at the Lantern, the best restaurant in town, enjoying the house special of prime rib.

"I don't know what I'll do now that you both are going back to your jobs," Grace said as they sipped their after dinner coffee.

"It's been a busy week. We sure appreciate all your help, Grace." Alison patted her hand.

"Family helps family," she snapped. "No need for thanks."

"Mom, I've been thinking," Ginny said slowly. "Let's not put the house on the market right away. I'm not ready to give it up just yet. I didn't realize how much I've missed it."

"I've been having second thoughts, too, honey. But what will we do with it? You have a job and an apartment, and so do I. I really hate to rent it out."

Before answering, Ginny was silent for a moment as she stared into her cup, running her finger around the rim. "I may want to get a teaching job here next semester. Being home this week has been an eye opener in many ways. I think I would like to live here, in our old home, for awhile. I can do some work on the house, and hire some out when I can afford it. What do you think?"

"I think it's the best idea you've ever had," chimed in Grace, clapping her hands in delight. "I'll have my girl right next door again."

"That's fine with me, honey, if it's what you want," Alison said with relief in her voice. She was pleased that Ginny would be living in their old house with Grace to keep a watchful eye. Now that Ginny knew about her birth, Alison felt like she was a little girl again and needed someone to watch out for her.

When Ginny pulled out of the driveway the next day, she smiled, knowing that she would return the first of June when the yellow climber on the front porch rail boasted its first buds.

When she arrived back at her apartment, she put everything away and quickly tidied up the mess that she had left. With a cup of hot tea in her hand, she sat on her sofa to rest. Looking about at the two tiny rooms, she felt claustrophobic after being in the roomy old house. She found herself pushing aside thoughts of her unfortunate beginnings and concentrated on what she could do to fix up her old home. Absorbed in her decorating books, she jumped when the phone broke the silence.

"Just checking to see that you got home okay," Alison said when Ginny picked up the receiver. "I enjoyed our time together, in spite of everything. Can I drive over for lunch next Saturday? We can talk about what you plan for the house. I'd like to help you."

"Sure, Mom. That would be fine."

By the time Ginny was through with that semester's teaching, she and her mother had a notebook full of ideas to bring the house up to date, and she was anxious to get started.

Leaving her children, though, was another matter. All her second graders were sad that she wouldn't be at the school anymore and gave her a little party. There were many hugs and sniffles when final good-byes were said. Her principal was not happy to see her go; she had been a very able teacher. Finally, the last few weeks were over, the u-haul was loaded with her meager belongings, and she made the drive home without incident.

Grace came over as she was starting to unload the u-haul.

"Let me help," she reached for the TV.

"No, Grace, that's too heavy for you."

"You picked it up, didn't you?" Grace answered back sharply.

"Yes, but my back knows it, too. I should have gotten some help."

"Miss Independent. Well, I'll be right back with some help. You just get the light boxes out, you hear?"

"Yes Ma'am." Ginny grinned. It would be sort of nice to have someone to look after her for a change. She took a box of towels inside and set them in the hall. When she came out, Grace had a denim clad young man by the sleeve.

"Ginny Lee, this is Noah Johnstone. He and his mother moved in across the street. Noah's on staff at the newspaper—a good reporter, too."

Ginny put out her hand, and found it squeezed by Noah's big one. She flinched.

"Sorry. I forget my own strength sometimes when I shake a lady's hand," he said in a slow southern drawl.

She took in the dark hair and eyes, olive skin, and beautiful white teeth smiling down at her from his over six-foot height.

Stammering a little, she stepped back. "I hope Grace hasn't taken you away from anything important. But we would appreciate your help."

"No problem. Where do you want things put?" he asked as he shouldered a box.

"Just line them up in the front hall. We'll unpack there."

"Nope. They're too heavy for you ladies. You just point to which room, and I'll deliver them," he insisted.

By the end of the day, things were reasonably straightened up and put away. A few small boxes remained for the next day. Grace had gone home to prepare a light supper. She had asked Noah and his mother to join them for chicken salad sandwiches. Ginny washed her face and hands and applied a little make-up before she crossed the yard to Grace's cheery red kitchen.

A frail looking woman with salt and pepper hair and huge dark eyes sat at the table talking to Grace as she prepared individual dinner plates. Noah stood by Grace, ready to take them from her and set them on the table. He smiled broadly at Ginny.

"Well, you don't look like you've spent the day moving. Ginny, this is my mother, Martha Johnstone." He set a heavily loaded plate down and put his hand on his mother's shoulder.

"Mrs. Johnstone," Ginny said, taking the woman's cold hand. Looking into her face, Ginny could see that she had once been lovely, and her broad smile was warm. It was obvious that Noah favored his mother with the same dark skin and eyes.

As they enjoyed their supper, Ginny learned that mother and son had returned to Martha Johnstone's hometown after she had become ill. Her brother and his family lived close by, and she wanted to be close to them. It was easy to see that Noah was devoted to his mother by the way he tended to her.

Later, while they were cleaning up, Grace told Ginny that Martha had only a short time left to live. "Cancer," she said with a shutter. "It seems to be striking all around us."

"How awful," Ginny replied, thinking of how her grandmother had suffered. "She seems like such a sweet person, and Noah seems totally devoted to her."

"He has been. They've only been here two months, but I've gotten to know them pretty well. They're nice folks," Grace said, adding with a smile. "So if he should ask you out, don't hesitate to accept."

Ginny burst into laughter. "You listened when we were standing on the porch, Miss Nosey. You heard him ask me out, and you heard me accept."

"Well, I just wanted you to know that it was okay. I approve." Grace snapped, turning up her nose and plunging her hands back in the dishwater. Ginny shook her head in amusement. It was wonderful to be around Grace again.

Ginny's first date with Noah was dinner and a movie. She found him so open and interesting to talk to that she told him all about her life over dinner, carefully leaving out anything about her father. She learned that Noah's father died two years before about the same time his mother was diagnosed with cancer.

"I wanted her to be here with my Uncle George and family. We left a lot of friends in Georgia, but she wanted to come back to her roots."

Ginny hesitated before asking, "Noah, how much longer do they give her, if you don't mind telling me?"

"Months, maybe a year, but that's a long shot. She feels good most of the time. The first round of chemo didn't work, so she chose to spend the rest of her time in peace. We see the doctor often, and he says she's doing remarkably well, considering. If she's in much pain, she doesn't let me know."

"It must be hard for you. Did you have to give up a good job to move back?"

"Not really. I like working for the paper here much better, and I really do like this town. Everyone is so friendly. Grace was on our doorstep with a pie the first day we were here."

Ginny nodded. "She would be, bless her."

"And I'm especially glad that we moved into this particular neighborhood, now more than ever." Noah smiled as he looked into Ginny's eyes.

"Me, too," she said, returning his gaze.

Chapter 7

It was the dream that woke her up. She had gone to bed dead tired after painting the front hall. Noah had come over to help after work or she could have never completed the job before midnight. She had fallen asleep immediately only to toss and turn, her aching muscles protesting every move.

She sat up and looked at the clock—almost five o'clock. Shadows, cast on the wall by the big oak, were fading into gray dawn. Scooting back down beneath the pale blue sheet, she closed her eyes and tried to recall every part of the dream that made her sit straight up in the bed, filled with anxiety.

She was in a room with a lot of people she didn't know. Pressing through the crowd was like pushing against a strong current. Her mother's face kept appearing, then disappearing in vivid flashes. She saw Grace on the other side of the room, dressed in one of her grandmother's old flannel robes. She called to her, but Grace didn't answer.

When the crowd fanned out and separated, she finally reached her friend who turned to her with a smile and said, "Ginny, this is your father." A tall young man her own age whirled around and reached out to shake her hand. "No, you're too young," she said in the dream. "I don't know you. You can't be my father." He turned and walked away, looking back at her once with gray-green eyes filled with sorrow. The dream faded. Only the face kept floating back to her, then receding; the face that was hers.

She tried to clear her mind and go back to sleep, but soon realized that she was awake for the day, so she picked up a book and tried to read for awhile. After reading the same page three times, she gave up. Throwing back the sheet, she slipped on her scuffs and went down to the kitchen to put on coffee. She looked out the window while the coffee dripped, filling the kitchen with its aroma.

Squirrels were scampering up and down the maple by the kitchen window. Birds were drinking from the birdbath her grandmother had placed in the flowerbed that was fast being taken over with weeds. A beautiful summer day should have filled her with energy. She had been energetic yesterday when she started on the painting, but there was only dejection this morning.

"Not enough sleep. Crazy dream," she murmured to herself. "I won't start anything today. I'll play hooky." After all, she and Noah had painted the front porch and the long hall that ran from front to back, and that was a major chore. Besides she promised to cook him dinner tonight.

Taking her coffee to the back porch, she watched the pink clouds layered over the horizon grow brighter as the sun began to disperse its first golden rays. She couldn't have seen this before from her tiny apartment. Her sense of depression lifted as she thought how happy she was with her decision to stay here. Her job at the elementary school was set; she had been hired on even before she actually moved. She had all summer to work on the house, or not, as the mood struck her.

Deciding it would be a good time to work in the flowerbeds before it got hot, she drained her coffee and went back to the laundry room. Taking her old work jeans and shirt off the peg where she had hung them the night before, she slipped them on, tossing her pajamas on the washer. Picking up trowel and gloves from the basket on the porch, she was soon engrossed in the battle of encroaching grass.

She stopped when she saw Grace stirring, and called for her to come over for coffee. Grace had a club meeting at ten o'clock, so their morning chat was brief, but pleasant. When Grace left, she forced herself back to the weeding and by eleven, she had all the beds free of crabgrass and unwanted wild violets. She fixed herself an early lunch, prepared as much of the dinner that she could do ahead, and took a warm soaking bath followed by a long nap. By the time she and Noah sat down at dinner, she felt like a different person.

"This was wonderful," he said to her as he polished off the remainder of her Southwest casserole. "I never did eat any lunch. I was out on a story all day, and I just forgot to eat."

"I skipped breakfast myself. I'll show you what I did in the back yard when we're through. What were you working on that was so engrossing that you forgot to eat?"

He told her of the story he was writing about a family reunion of four brothers who hadn't seen each other for thirty years. "Cam took the pictures—he's a wonderful photographer. It will come out in the weekend paper. It was an emotional thing to watch, seeing a family come together again. We both had lumps in our throats, Cam and I, but we tried hard to be professional and detached."

Ginny smiled. "I can see that side of you. You're very sensitive. I like that in a person."

"I'm glad. I think you're very much that way, too, under that front you put on sometimes."

"Why would you say that about me, Noah? You really don't know me that well."

He reached for her hand. "I can sense this barrier, Ginny. We've told each other about our childhoods, but you've never mentioned your father, except to say that he was 'gone'. Sometimes I feel tenseness in you when you talk about your mother." He pulled his hand away and shrugged. "I'm sorry. None of this is any of my business. But we're becoming such good friends. I think of you when I'm at work, and I look forward to coming home and seeing you out in the yard, or helping you on the house…"

"No, you're right," she interrupted. "There is something, something that I just learned a few weeks ago. I haven't told anyone about it, and it is bothering me. I feel close enough to you to tell you about it, if you want to listen to family problems."

He pushed back his chair. "Thanks for trusting me. Let's take our iced tea to the porch and get comfortable."

They settled on the porch, and she told him the story about her parents that she only recently learned. He listened, occasionally running his finger up and down the back of her hand that was clenched tightly on the arm of the chair. When she finished, she laughed nervously and said, "So that's my story."

He rose and stood in front of her, pulling her to her feet. She went into his arms, and he rested his chin on the top on her head. She breathed in the smell of bath soap and cologne and the fabric softener in his shirt. Tightening her arms around his waist, she felt like she could stay in the circle of his arms all day.

He swayed slightly, holding her until she relaxed in his arms. She was a perfect fit, nestled against him. It had been a long time since he had felt this close to a woman. When she began to slowly pull back, he wanted to grab her and hold her tightly again, but he let her go. They sat back down, smiling a little nervously.

"Thank you," she said, "for listening. It felt good to get it out in the open."

"So what are you going to do?" He leaned toward her and looked intently into her eyes.

"Do?"

"I mean, do you want to look for him?"

"Goodness, no. I've lived all my life without him. Why would I want to look for him?" She bristled a little at the suggestion.

"If I'd fathered a child—and believe me, I haven't—I would want to know. I would want that person to find me."

"Bad idea. You haven't met my mother. Her reaction to that idea would be—I'm not sure what it would be–anger, I suspect."

"But what about him? He certainly did a bad thing to your mother. But maybe, just maybe, if he'd known about you, he would have wanted to marry her."

"She was too hurt to want marriage with him, I'm sure."

"It sounds as if she didn't try very hard to find him. Not taking his side or anything, but he must have been just a kid himself. He may have been scared to run away like he did. If that were common behavior for him, he would probably have been too cocky to run off. He could have just denied it or blamed her. Lots of guys have done that and gotten away with it."

"Possibly. I hadn't looked at it from his side at all. But he could have found my mother easily if he wanted to make amends."

"That was a terrible thing he did. But she had you, and it sounds like she and your grandmother loved you very much and gave you the most normal childhood they could." His voice was low and soft.

"Yes, they did the best they knew how. We were so close," she said as tears welled up in her eyes at the thought of Laura Belle. "I'm sorry you didn't get to meet my grandmother. She was quite a lady."

"But I'm glad that I finally got to know, really know, her granddaughter." He rose again and looked down at her. "Do you suppose we could put on some music so I would have an excuse to hold you again? That was kinda nice."

She cocked her head coyly and gave him her hand. "Who needs music?" she asked as he pulled her back into his arms, humming a nameless tune as they moved slowly across the porch floor.

Chapter 8

The minister's deep booming voice closed the prayer. "…And guide us through the week as we go about our pursuits. Keep us always close to thee. In Jesus holy name, Amen." Before the prayer's end, Alison's thoughts strayed to her daughter so lovely beside her in her gauzy green summer dress. Ginny seemed different this weekend, more relaxed, calmer. They had spent the day before shopping, laughing, and enjoying each other. It was one of the best weekends they spent together in a long time. She wondered how much the change in mood was due to the handsome young neighbor.

Ginny had suggested that they invite Grace, Noah, and Martha over for breakfast Saturday morning before their shopping spree, and Alison liked both Noah and his mother immediately. She especially appreciated how good Noah was to his mother. And Grace, dear Grace, kept sending her signals by winking when Ginny wasn't looking.

"Mom, service is over," Ginny whispered.

Alison jerked her head up as she realized that she was still standing with bowed head though the rest of the congregation was moving toward the doors. She smiled ruefully. "My mind wandered," she said, following her daughter down the isle.

Noah greeted them at the front of the church. "He's very handsome," Alison thought. In gray pants and a cream linen jacket, he reminded her a little of another young man in another time.

"Is your mom not feeling well this morning?" Ginny asked.

"No. She woke up feeling weak, so she stayed in bed. She's due to go back for tests tomorrow. Say a little prayer for her." He turned to Alison. "I'm glad we got to meet, Ms. Cantrell. And I'm glad your daughter decided to come back here to live. I like being her neighbor." He smiled at Ginny, and Alison caught the look that passed between them. "They're falling in love," she thought, and her heart felt glad.

Later, settled in the red booths of the Chinese buffet, she couldn't resist asking Ginny about her relationship with Noah.

"My goodness, Mother. Ask me in about six months and I'll tell you. We've only known each other three weeks."

"I didn't mean to be nosy, but I couldn't help but notice the way he looked at you this morning."

Ginny grinned. "And just how did Noah look at me?"

"Like you were a steak and he was a starving man!"

Ginny chuckled, playfully slapping her mother's hand. "You have the greatest imagination; Grammy always said that about you. We've gone out some, but mostly he's helped me with painting and the yard. And we eat together sometimes, his mother included, on occasion. But to answer you're unasked question—yes, I do like him a lot."

"Good. I'm glad to hear it." Alison speared a piece of baby corn and pointed her fork at Ginny. "You haven't had a serious boyfriend since...when? I can't even remember."

"Well, there was Anthony Gordon in my second year of college. You do remember Anthony, don't you?" Ginny rolled her eyes upward.

Alison chuckled. "Poor Anthony. He was such a mama's boy. I was so glad that blew over."

"Yeah, his mother called me after our third date and told me I was interfering with his studies. Didn't take me long to figure out he wasn't worth having to deal with her."

Just then, an old friend of Alison's stopped by their table to chat for a moment, and Ginny watched her mother during the exchange. She looked so much younger than her friend, her dark skin clear and unlined. At forty-three, she could have passed for thirty-three. Ginny felt suddenly sad that her mother had chosen to remain single all these years. She should have been happily married, perhaps had more children. Visions of a sister drifted through Ginny's mind, one who was close in age and could be sitting here with the two of them right now. She tried to imagine what she would have looked like, this unborn sister.

When the friend left, Ginny worked up the courage to ask her mother a question that had been on her mind. "Mom, something has been bothering me. I hope you'll forgive me for asking this, but…why didn't you look for my father?"

"I told you, honey. My friend, Paul, talked to John's parents, and they hadn't heard from him since he left college. How could I find him, and why would I want to?"

"I don't know. Maybe if he knew about me, he would…I mean, shouldn't he have been told about me?"

Sighing, Alison twisted her napkin on her lap. "I didn't want him to have any claim on you. You forget how hurt I was. And your grandmother would have had him in court, if she knew where he was. I didn't want that."

"But, Mom. That's just what he deserved, wasn't it?"

"Even though I was angry and miserable, I felt like what he did was partly my fault. I was so inexperienced with men, and…I still had feelings for him, even though I denied it to them and to myself, too. It was such a confusing time, Ginny."

Ginny wanted to pursue it, but seeing the pain in her mother's face, she said, "I know, Mom. We won't talk about it anymore." She reached for her hand. "Let's enjoy the few hours we have before you drive back home." Alison smiled and nodded, relieved to drop the subject. Every time it came up she felt defensive and sad.

Later, when her mother had gone and she was alone at home, Ginny wandered through the house, restlessly arranging pillows and straightening pictures. Eventually, she pulled out the heavy wallpaper book on loan from the paint store and took it to the dining room table. Looking for new wallpaper was something she had begun to enjoy since moving back in the house, but tonight she lost interest quickly.

Her mind kept darting back to her conversation with Noah about her father. Her mother had done the best she could under the circumstances. Yet, she got the feeling from what little was said earlier that Alison regretted not looking for John. How different would life have been if he had been told he had a child on the way? Or would he have just denied paternity and hurt her more? What kind of person was he now? Where did he live? Did he have a family? Did she have siblings? She slammed the book closed just as the phone rang.

"Hi. How was your weekend with your mother?" Noah asked.

"Oh, it was good," she answered, trying not to sound giddy at the sound of his voice. "We shopped yesterday, and she made me my favorite chicken casserole last night. In fact, I can't remember when we had a better time together. How's your mother feeling tonight?"

"Better. She stayed in bed until afternoon, then got up and seemed invigorated again. She's in her bedroom engrossed in a book right now."

"Good." She paused, searching for the right words. "Listen, Noah, I think I may need your help after all. I've been thinking–I may want to locate my father. Not meet him or anything—definitely not that–but locate him, find out something about him, you know? I have no idea how to go about it. Since you work at the paper, I thought you might…"

"I'll be right there." She heard the phone click, and in less that a minute he was ringing the doorbell.

Chapter 9

The next morning as she awoke and snuggled back down under the cover, Ginny began to have second thoughts about having asked Noah to help her find her father. To begin with, she had little information for him to go on. And he was such a busy person with his job and his sick mother to look after. She asked him to help her on impulse, and normally she wasn't an impulsive person.

If he did find her father, what would she do with the information? Would she go to him and say, "Hi. I'm your long lost daughter?" Shaking her head at her foolish thoughts, she reached for her robe. No, that would certainly not be her approach. What if she just got a glimpse of him? Or did she really just want to know where he was and what his life was like?

She sat down at her dressing table and ran a brush through her hair. Green eyes looked back at her from the mirror, the color she inherited from her father.

Auburn hair sprang from the brush and curled around her ears, the color must be from him. Something inside her longed to see him. But at a distance. How would she accomplish that? Spy around corners? Follow him in a taxi?

"You've seen too much TV lately," she said to her reflection with a smirk.

Rising, she pulled back the curtain. Noah was backing out of his driveway, and she could see Martha in the car with him. She said a quick prayer that the tests would show that Martha would have more time to spend with her son. Losing his mother would be so hard on Noah. He had already lost one parent.

By the end of the day she had ordered wallpaper for the dining room, given the house a quick going over, and re-organized the kitchen pantry. Fairly satisfied with her day, she went across the street to see how Martha fared with her tests. She found her in the kitchen preparing supper.

"Please let me help you," Ginny begged. "You must be tired after such a long day."

"No, honey. We're having leftovers, and I'm just warming up. But I'd love it if you would have a cup of tea with me."

They sat at the kitchen table, sipping their tea quietly. Martha reached over and patted Ginny's hand.

"You're so sweet to pay me so much attention, Ginny. I'm glad you're here for Noah, too. He thinks so much of you."

"You have a wonderful son. He must have been raised right to be as compassionate and kind as he is."

"Thanks. We tried. Noah was an easy child to raise. But he's had a lot of sickness around him, with his father and now me. That's why I want to be as strong as possible, at least to seem strong, and do everything I can for as long as I can."

"Did you get any results from your tests today?" Ginny asked softly.

"Yes, actually they looked pretty good. The doctor says I'm doing very well right now. He was a little upset with me because I chose not to do the chemo thing again, but I think I've convinced him that gaining three or four months is not worth the suffering, for me, at least."

Ginny looked at the frail but still beautiful face and saw the strength of her son. "You're brave, Martha. I don't know what I would have done."

"No one does until they go through it. Ah, here's Noah with my prescription. Will you stay for a bite, Ginny? As I said, it's leftovers, but there's plenty."

Ginny bent and pressed her cheek. "Thanks, but I promised Grace I'd eat dinner with her tonight. And I'd better scoot or she'll be coming after me. I'll talk to you tomorrow." She turned a little shyly to Noah.

He wove his fingers through hers. "Have a good day?"

"Super. How about you?"

"I guess Mom told you the tests were good. That was a relief. Now I have to eat and get back to the paper. We're getting out a special edition this weekend, and we're all putting in extra hours."

"See you tomorrow then," she said, squeezing his hand as she turned. Again she felt guilty for taking up his time with her hair-brained scheme. He had so much to do.

"Well, your salad has about wilted, young lady," Grace complained as Ginny walked in her back door.

"Sorry, Grace. I went over to see how Martha was doing after her tests today."

"Oh, that's right, I'd forgotten about that. How was she?"

"Feeling pretty good. The tests turned out okay, at least, for now. She's such a sweet lady."

"Yes, she is. And Noah's not so bad either, is he, Ginny?" Grace cocked her head and grinned.

"No, he's not bad at all, Grace. Now where's the spaghetti you promised me? I'm starved!"

"Don't be evasive with me, Missy! I know you two are keeping company."

Ginny laughed. "Keeping company? Really, Grace!"

"Well, that's what they used to call it," Grace replied with a huff. "Now sit down here and tell me all about him, or I'll tell your mother how bad you're being the next time she's here."

Ginny grabbed the tiny woman and hugged her. "Oh, I'm so glad to be here again, even if I do have to put up with you!"

"Well, you always were a lucky girl!"

Grace convinced Ginny to call a professional to wallpaper the dining room with the tall ceilings, so when Ginny got home, she went over her remodeling budget carefully. If she did that, some other improvements would have to wait, but she decided it was worth it. She called Mr. Casey, who fortunately wasn't busy, and he agreed to do the job when the paper came in. It came in on Wednesday, and Thursday morning Mr. Casey and his helper were putting up the paper. They were done in one long day, and Ginny was vacuuming the rug when Noah came over looking weary.

"What a week!" He exclaimed. "But the special is ready to go to press—at least my part of it is." He pulled her to him. "I've missed seeing you this week. I know it's late, but I couldn't wait to talk to you."

She smiled and wrapped her arms around him even tighter. Finally, she pulled away. "I've missed you, too. Come sit and tell me what you wrote. Better still, you sit, and I'll bring you a big glass of iced tea. Then we'll talk."

She fixed two glasses, and they sat in the porch swing. The sliver of a moon hung above the oak, and the tree frogs were humming noisily. The thump of dog paws on the wood steps brought Grover, the golden retriever from down the street, on his routine evening prowl. After getting his petting fix and sniffing around for food, he jumped from the porch, moving like a yellow ghost under the street light.

"Sweet dog. I'd love to have one just like him," Ginny murmured.

"He seems to live all over the neighborhood. Mom feeds him sometimes. Umm. This is good tea. What's in it?"

"It's fruit tea, has several juices in it."

They drifted quietly in the swing, contented. Then he reached for her hand. "Ginny, I think I found your father."

She stopped the motion of the swing, and he felt her hand tremble in his. "Already? How were you able to find him so quickly?"

"It was a fluke, really. My boss has a brother who works at the college where your parents went to school."

"He doesn't know...I mean..."

"No, he's not from here, and the name meant nothing to him. Don't worry. No one knows why we're trying to find him."

"Where is he?" Her voice shook with emotion.

"After getting his social security number, it was just a matter of working contacts by computer. Luckily there weren't very many people with the same middle name—it's Patterson—a family name, I guess. We traced him to Ventura, California, then to Laurel Springs, Virginia."

She jumped up in amazement. "I've been there. It's just across the border up in the mountains. Some girlfriends and I went up for a weekend when I was in school. It's an artsy little Victorian town, very old." She sat back down, and her voice trailed off as she remembered the winding streets, little shops and cottages. She looked at Noah, her eyes wide. "I could have passed him on the street and not even have known it."

Pulling her arm through his, he continued. "He and his wife run a bed and breakfast called 'Calley's Cottage', and he's never been in trouble with the law or anything like that, as far as we could see."

"How could you have found all that so fast?" she repeated.

"Newspapers have their ways. I'm pretty sure he's the one, Ginny. Chances of a mistake are small."

They sat in silence for a moment. Then she turned to him. "I don't know how to thank you, Noah. I didn't expect to find him, really, thought it would be harder to locate someone. It's amazing—and a little scary, too. Don't know what I'll do about it yet, but I want you to know how much I appreciate all your trouble."

"And I want you to know that there's nothing I wouldn't do for you, Ginny," he said huskily. She took his face in her hands and kissed him slowly and gently.

He groaned. "If I don't leave now…um, yeah, I'd better. Goodnight, Sweet Ginny." Rising, he pulled her to him for a hug, releasing her quickly, and ran down the steps.

Collapsing back down in the swing with a sigh, Ginny put her hand to her chest. She had fallen in love with Noah, and she had found her father. She wasn't sure which was making her heart beat out of control the most.

Chapter 10

For three days, she told herself that she wouldn't go to Laurel Springs. Her brain told her that she didn't really want to know anything about John Fredericks. She should hate him forever for what he did and let it go at that. But, deep inside, another part of her wanted to see him, to let him know she existed. The third night, she quit arguing with herself and decided that she had to go, for her own sanity. Her plans were to rise early and take off for Laurel Springs before she could change her mind again.

Unfortunately, she lost a filling during dinner, so the next morning found her on the phone with the dentist. It seemed he could work her in about one in the afternoon, and she had no choice but to take it. She packed her car, planning to leave right from the office.

It was almost three when she set off in a nervous, anxious state, plus a numb jaw. To get her mind off the reason for her trip, she took the back roads instead of the parkway so she would have beautiful scenery to distract her. She began to relax as she traveled further down the two lane road. The warm afternoon sun was soothing, and she rolled down her window to catch the smells of the countryside; the animals, piney woods, the honeysuckle along the fencerows.

She wished Noah could have come with her. And he would have except for an emergency in his department—an early arrival of his assistant's baby. He made her promise to call every night she was gone and insisted that if she really needed him at any hour, he would drop everything, regardless.

Chuckling to herself, she recalled telling Grace earlier that she would be gone for a few days.

"You're going by yourself?" Grace asked with a frown. "Why don't I go with you? I'd love to go to Laurel Springs. Haven't been there in years. Won't take me but a minute to throw some things together."

"Thanks for the offer, Grace, but I really need to be by myself for a few days. Got a lot to think about, you know."

"You mean Noah?" She bent forward with bright eyes and whispered. "Has he asked you to marry him?"

She had laughed at her long time neighbor. "No, Grace. You're such a romantic. Honestly, I just like to be alone sometimes. I have my school year to plan and things to buy for my classroom, and just need a little change of scenery, that's all."

"Huh! Young women shouldn't go off by themselves these days, too dangerous!" she had grumbled. "Okay, but you be careful, you hear? And stay in a nice safe place, not in some dump just to save money."

"Yes, Ma'am," she had answered as she tossed her make-up case in the back of the jeep and waved good-bye.

With two more driving hours ahead of her, two hours to wonder if she was doing the right thing, she pulled over and went through her audiotapes. Putting on one of her favorites, she blocked out her fears and uncertainties about her trip and became absorbed in the smooth reading of the book. However, she eventually realized that she was lost in her own thoughts again and had to keep rewinding the tape to keep up with the story.

Soon the narrow mountain road began twisting upward, and the sign told her Laurel Springs was just ahead. Everything looked almost the same as it had three years before when she had driven up with classmates. There were a couple of new motels on the winding street before making the turn to the historic district. One motel was nestled down in the trees, and she felt that it could be her home for the night if there were a vacancy. But first she was going to drive through the historic section of town.

Laurel Springs had been known in the early 1900's for its mineral springs. People came from far away to have their aches and pains, or their serious diseases, cured by the waters. Like many such bustling towns at the turn of the century, it grew less and less of a vacation spot as times grew harder. After both World Wars, when things were booming elsewhere, the little town slept in its isolated backwoods.

However, the locals still held on to their homes and kept them up as best they could, depending on whatever local work there was to do. Then in the 50's and 60's, the town began to boom again. Victorian houses were brought back to life and new cottages were built, sometimes on a mere sliver of land. Baths were opened again, shops moved in; artisans began plying their trades. There were still springs all through the town, but they were blocked off with brick or concrete barriers so the public could still see but not drink from them. Now, only the large main bathhouse remained, remodeled, with sauna and massage therapies.

The town itself, with its stores and Victorian houses, was built on the side of the mountain, and all the streets wove around and up. At the very top sat the big hotel, over a century old, a huge stone structure with its turrets rising possessively over the town like a castle rising above its surfdom.

As she drove along with the very slow traffic through the downtown, she saw that her favorite shops were still there. Hermione's, with its unusual clothing and accessories was in the same place, as was The Nature Place. There she had fallen in love with the beautiful hand-painted and stained ducks of all kinds and the furniture made from deer horns.

But she didn't stop to do any shopping and instead headed up the hill to Summer Street that provided a balcony view above the downtown section. The lovely houses were painted in every color imaginable, some in four or five shades. Some had bed and breakfast signs in front, and others were private homes. Before she had been here in the fall when the leaves were all over the streets and the air smelled smoky. Today the trees were lush and green and flowers bloomed in every yard and hung in baskets from every porch.

Ginny was so enthralled with the charming street that she almost forgot to look for the sign 'Calley's Cottage'. She wound over to Gardenia Lane. Driving slowly along the narrow street, she noticed that none of the houses had signs here except for the one that had a 'Weddings and Receptions' sign in front. She pulled over and stopped to admire its maroon, blue and pink colors on the wide gingerbread covered porch.

After looking the town over, she still hadn't found 'Calley's Cottage', so she returned to the small motel and got a back room, surrounded by trees. She went through the phone book the very first thing, but there was no listing for 'Calley's Cottage' or for a John Fredericks. After settling into the modest but comfortable room, she stepped out onto the small porch that overlooked a wooded ravine. The air was degrees cooler, so she sat for awhile and listened to the cacophony of birds.

She had a sinking feeling that she had come all this way for nothing. Since he wasn't in the phonebook, it was quite likely that he had moved on. Perhaps he had died, and she would never be able to confront him with her discovery. Her heart felt heavy with disappointment.

Sighing, she realized that it was growing late and she needed to eat. Having passed a German restaurant on the way in, she decided to have dinner there. Before leaving, she walked up to the office and inquired about

'Calley's Cottage'. The friendly clerk handed her a list of the local bed and breakfasts, and she leaned against the counter, the paper trembling as her eyes ran slowly down the pages. There was no listing for it there, either.

Smiling, she handed the list back to the pretty lady. "I'd heard of that place, and I wanted particularly to find that one. Have you ever heard of it?"

"There are so many, dear. They stay in business for awhile, then sell out or buy another and change names. Let me see if I have an old list in the file. Just a moment." She rummaged through a filing cabinet off to the side and came up with another list. "Let's see. Tell me the name again?"

"Calley's Cottage." Ginny repeated.

"Oh, yes, I remember that one. It's here on this list. But I doubt if it's still operating or it would be on the current one."

"Could you give me the address?" Ginny asked, with a tremor in her voice.

"Here, you can have this. It's out of date. You'll probably find that it's been closed and converted back to a private home or an antique shop."

"Thanks. Oh, by the way, is the German restaurant out on the highway a good place to eat?"

"Yes, indeed. If you like German food, it's the best."

Ginny thanked her, put the list in her purse, and headed out to Mueller's Taste of Old Germany with a lighter heart. Maybe she wasn't wasting her time after all. It was dark now, and she couldn't do much until tomorrow, so she decided to relax and enjoy her dinner.

The place was crowded, but the atmosphere was nice, complete with native costumed waiters. In spite of her state of nerves, she ordered potato pancakes stuffed with creamed spinach and vegetables, and the service was prompt. The food was delicious, and, still hungry, she ordered apple strudel for dessert. As she finished her coffee, she had an urge to seek out the address immediately, but reason dictated that it might be hard to find it in the dark winding streets, so she returned to the motel.

She walked out on her tiny porch and called Noah on her cell phone.

"Hi. How are you and what's going on?" His voice soothed her instantly.

"Well, I have the address of 'Calley's Cottage', but it looks like it may be out of business. It wasn't listed on the current lists of bed and breakfasts nor is it in the phonebook. I'm going to see if I can find it tomorrow. The motel clerk seemed to think it's not in business anymore." She paused and sighed. "I wish you were here."

"I wish I were, too. I wish I'd told my boss I was taking off, period. Listen, if things get scary for you, or anything happens where you feel threatened or need support, you call me. I'll leave the paper and be there as fast as I can, job or no job. Hear me, Ginny?"

"I'll call whenever I know something."

"Promise?"

"Promise."

"I miss you."

"Me, too."

When they hung up, she felt terribly lonesome and sat numbly on the porch until the chill drove her back in. She pulled the list from her purse and stared at it. Calley's Cottage–25 Tulip Lane. Tomorrow she would find the house. Would she find HIM? Could he have become an alcoholic? A drug abuser? Her imagination was running away with her. Suddenly she felt cold waves of panic sweep over her. For a little bit, she would drive back home right now.

No, she wouldn't let herself think that way; she had come too far now. She washed her face in warm water, slathered on some moisturizer, put on her pajamas, and turned on the TV. Tomorrow was the day she would seek out her father. If she didn't find him, she would go home and put this search out of her mind. Settling herself on the pillows with the remote in hand, Ginny made a comfy nest for what might be a very long night.

Chapter 11

She showered and dressed, stopping off at the office for a quick cup of coffee and a bite of breakfast. Her stomach was in knots, so she forced herself to take her time and have some juice and toast. She picked up a map from the desk and went over it as she sipped a second cup. Then, with a deep breath, she walked out into the bright morning sun and pulled out of the parking space into the morning traffic. The time for action was here.

Tulip Lane veered off from the circle around the old hotel. The street dropped steeply, then flattened out and curved around to intersect with Summer Street. She drove slowly down the incline, looking at house numbers, until she came to the point where the street began to even out. There it was, a yellow cottage trimmed in hunter green and rose, its house numbers in bold black above the door.

She stopped the car a little past the house on the opposite side and rolled down her window. Her mind was in a whirl, and her hands, fiercely gripping the steering the wheel, were icy cold. Rubbing them together, she forced herself to study the exterior of the house. A porch with 'carpenter's lace' extended across the front. The small yard had once been flowers bordered by river stones, and a few perennials still struggled to survive. She could make out the remains of tulips and a mass of lavender that was still standing proudly. There was a signpost in the yard, but the sign had been taken down, and the paint on the post was peeling.

Getting out of her car on shaky legs, she walked further down the street and crossed, then proceeded to walk back toward the cottage so as not to be obvious. It was bigger than it looked. She could see from the side view that it was a long house with a basement on the back side of the steep lot. Just as she came even with the gate, the front door opened and a man with a watering can walked out on the porch. Startled, she turned her head, but not before she noticed that his hair was auburn. She stopped, pretending to look in her purse, but trying to get glimpses of the man. His face was obscured as he went about his task.

Without seeming to notice her, he watered the two hanging baskets of pink geraniums, pausing to pinch off a dead bloom or two. Then he poured the rest of the water on the spindly hydrangea by the steps. Ginny turned boldly to get a better look at him, but only saw his back as he opened the door and went back in.

Crossing the street to her car, she fumbled with the door, her knees so weak that she practically fell into the seat. She uncapped a bottle of water and took a long drink. It had been in the car all night and was warm, and she made a face as she put the cap back on with trembling fingers. She sat until her hands stopped shaking and her breath became even. In spite of the fear that still rattled her nerves and knotted her stomach, she steeled herself into action. She could either wait until the man came out again, in which case she would ask directions, or she could walk up to the door and ask if there was a room available. She couldn't think of any other ploy.

She put her sunglasses back on, took a deep breath, and got out of the car. She paused at the gate, fighting a strong impulse to flee. Instead she walked briskly up the short walk, up the steps, and onto the porch. There her knees grew weak again, and she almost turned back. But she knocked on the door before her fear could make her retreat.

She knocked twice before he opened the door. "Yes?"

He was of medium height, slender, and his body seemed to list to one side. Somehow she had expected a much taller man. But his green eyes were clear, and the auburn hair was beginning to gray around the temples. He looked at her, waiting for a reply, then added; "Can I help you?"

She stammered a few words, and then cleared her throat. "Excuse me. I was wondering if you had any rooms available."

"What makes you think I have rooms?"

She pulled the out of date list from her purse. "Isn't this 25 Tulip Lane? Calley's Cottage?"

He looked down at his feet as he replied softly. "Yes, but I'm no longer in business. Sorry." He stepped back as if to close the door.

"Oh, dear. Everything is full up." The lie slipped out smoothly. "I thought it would be easy to find a bed and breakfast with so many in town. But all are booked ahead. You're the last one I tried."

"Miss, have you tried the motels? There are a number of them on the highway, and this early in the summer I doubt they would be full." He spoke softly to her, and it boosted her courage.

"But they are...or some of them are, anyway. I didn't come here to stay at a motel. I had my heart set on a bed and breakfast. I only have a few days off from work, and I don't want to stay by myself in an old motel with all these beautiful homes around here to stay in." She smiled her brightest smile, realizing that her lip was twitching. He must have taken it for the beginning of tears because he paused and looked into her strangely familiar face.

He began to explain in a kind voice. "I haven't been in the business for months now. I wish I could help you, but, you see, I'm here by myself and don't have anyone to assist me. If you'd like, I can get on the phone and see if anybody else has an extra room."

"No," she said sharply. "I mean, I've already tried. I guess I'll just have to drive on home. It wouldn't be any fun to tell my friends that I had to stay in a motel."

He stepped out onto the porch, revealing a limp as he moved. Sighing, he said, patiently, "Have you been up to the big hotel on the hill? They usually have plenty of rooms. They're a bit expensive, but if you like history and old décor, you'd like it. They've just restored it to its original state. It's quite beautiful."

She peered at him through her sunglasses. She wasn't sure, in spite of his coloring, that he was her father. Quickly, she put out her hand. "I'm Olivia Summers from . er. . Nashville, Tennessee."

Smiling slightly, he shook her hand. "John Fredericks."

Her heart did a flip in her chest, and she felt like she might faint. She swallowed down the bile that threatened to rise in her throat. It was really John, the man who she had wondered about for so many weeks; the man who was her father. Her hand shook as she withdrew from the handshake. She must not let the moment pass. "Is there no way you could rent me a room? Just for one night? I promise I won't be any trouble. I am not feeling very well, and I just can't think about driving all the way home right now. It's such a long drive."

He frowned and scratched his head. "You are persistent." Then, in a softer voice, he said, "I'm sorry you don't feel well. Why don't you sit down here in the rocker and let me get you something. Water? How about a glass of lemonade?"

"Lemonade would be wonderful, if it's no trouble." She nearly fell into the wicker rocker and looked back at him sheepishly. He went back in the house, and she let out a big sigh of relief. He hadn't gotten her off the premises yet. Wiping perspiration from her forehead, she drew deep breaths to settle her rolling stomach.

He quickly returned with a glass of cold lemonade and sat across from her in a matching porch chair. Smiling, she drank deeply, and then set the glass on the wicker table between them. "Thank you so much. This is delicious." She opened her purse and took out a bottle of aspirin and downed two with the lemonade.

He watched her warily. "Are you going to be okay?"

"I hope so. It's just these dizzy spells–inner ear, I guess. I hate to drive when they come on me."

"No, that's not a good idea. Look, if you don't mind the mess, I can give you a room, just for one night. As I told you, I've not been an innkeeper for awhile, and I don't have a housekeeper. If you don't have any qualms about staying here alone, I can fix you up with a room, just to help you out."

"Oh, that would be wonderful. Thank you so much."

He rose. "Do you have a bag?"

"Yes, in the car across the street."

"If you'll give me your key, I'll get the bag and lock your car. It will be okay there."

Was there anything in the car that would give her away? The tag on her luggage; would he notice that? Her hand shook as she handed him the key. He moved quickly and returned with her bag and motioned her into the house in front of him. She swallowed down a stab of fear, realizing that she would be alone in this house with a man whom she really didn't know.

"Straight down the hall to the left," he said, limping behind her.

She got a glimpse of a cozy living room with quaint white furniture and muted flowered pillows and curtains. The long hall was lined with family pictures in large old-fashioned frames. She turned into the room, and he set her bag on a luggage rack.

"It's dusty, but otherwise clean," he said, apologetically, as he opened the shutters to let in the sunlight. "Since it's getting on to lunchtime, I'll open a can of soup for you and let you get some rest. You'll be on your own for supper. If you don't feel like going out, I'll order in for you."

"Oh, I didn't mean to be this much trouble," she murmured.

"It's no trouble. It'll be good to have someone to talk to for a change." He smiled at her as he pulled the door to. She had the feeling that he was sincere, that he was glad that she was here.

Ginny sank down on the bed. Here she was in the same house with the man who fathered her. What to do now? She hadn't expected to get this far. She would just have to play it by ear. But somehow, in the next twenty-four hours, she would have to reveal her reason for being here. Would he believe her? Would he be angry at being discovered? Turning, she laid back on the pile of pillows, rubbing her forehead. She really did have a doozy of a headache now.

Chapter 12

A little later, he brought a tray to her room with soup, crackers, and iced tea. Ginny, still wearing her sunglasses, took the tray and thanked him. He stood outside her door, looking at her with concern in his eyes.

"I hope this makes you feel better. Call if you need anything else. I imagine that you'll be wise to just rest this afternoon. Maybe the dizziness will pass. Do the sunglasses help your headache?"

She nodded, pushing them tighter against her face.

"Well, as I said, call if you need anything. And just leave your tray outside when you're finished," he said as he closed the door.

Ginny ate the soup. Although she found it difficult to swallow, she didn't want to leave uneaten food after all his trouble. After she sat the empty tray in the hall, she looked around the room, really seeing it for the first time. The high bed was walnut with a spindle legged side table. The walls had been done in a pale blue wash, and the blue and white quilt with pillows in blues and yellows definitely echoed a woman's touch. Blue and white ceramics and plates adorned shelves and walls, and the tiny bath had blue and yellow towels. All was covered with a fine layer of dust.

She wondered why he was living here alone. Did he and his wife divorce? Though there were no personal items in the room, it had a homey feel. Sometime in the afternoon, she would slip out into the hall and look at the pictures she saw hanging there. Maybe there would be clues about this man who was her father. But for now, the bed looked inviting, and she had the whole afternoon to spend in this room because of her 'illness'.

Last night had been spent going over every possible scenario that could take place when she revealed her identity. She had tossed and turned, waking up from brief bursts of sleep to imagine his reaction, and her own. Now, with the soft featherbed calling to her, she kicked off her shoes, nestled among the pillows, and was soon fast asleep from sheer exhaustion. She awoke when the late afternoon sun played across her face.

She slept so hard that she was disoriented for a second or two. Then the anxiety of her position returned, and she lay there not knowing what to do next. Getting up, she brushed her teeth. There were still circles under her eyes, and she touched them up with fresh make-up and ran a comb through her hair, still damp from the pillow.

An hour later, he knocked on her door. "Miss.. er..Summers? Hope I'm not disturbing you."

"No," she answered shakily through the door.

"I'm going to order pizza for myself tonight, and I wondered if you might like me to order enough for you. You may feel like going out, and there are many good places to eat if you do. I just thought I'd check."

"Pizza would be fine, Mr. Fredericks," she answered.

"It usually takes about forty five minutes so I usually order early. I'll call you, and we can eat on the porch— that is, unless you'd rather eat in your room."

"No, the porch would be nice. And thank you." She sat in the wicker rocker and heard his footsteps as he walked down the hall. This was the perfect opportunity. She had to confront him; there would never be a better time. She rocked and looked at her watch nervously until she heard him call, "Pizza's here."

She put on her sunglasses and opened her door. He was standing in the hall with pizza boxes in his hands. "Back this way." He led her to a screened porch that seemed to be sitting in the treetops. A patio table was already set with paper plates and glasses of ice. Cans of coke sat in a wicker carrier, and a pitcher of iced tea sat in the middle of the table.

"I have pepperoni and double cheese, hope you like one of them," he smiled as he took the pies from their cartons.

"Both," she replied.

"Good. Help yourself to coke or tea and the pizza of your choice." He seemed jovial and pleased to have her company. She relaxed a little, as she poured her tea and reached for a piece of pizza.

"Um, this hits the spot," she said, trying really hard to enjoy her food. As they ate, they chatted about the town, and he gave her a brief history about the springs along with "cure" stories that had been circulated for a century. He laughed as he told her about the many bathers who swore they had been cured of everything from tuberculosis to acne. When there was a lag in the conversation, she knew she had to ask him questions about himself, so she took a deep breath and began.

"Mr. Fredericks, I don't mean to be nosy, but why did you give up inn keeping? This is such a lovely place to stay."

He sat his can of coke down and said nothing for a moment. She was about to panic until he answered in a slow deep voice.

"For some reason, I feel like I've known you longer than one day. I don't know why. Anyway, I don't mind telling you. Ten years ago, I moved here with my wife, Sherrill, and our daughter, Calley. We had been here for a vacation, and we loved the town. I was tired of my job as a banker and wanted to try something new. So we bought this place and opened up a bed and breakfast."

"So the cottage was named for your daughter?"

He dropped his head a little and continued. "Yes. As I said we loved it here, and we did well as innkeepers. Sherrill was a free lance writer, so she took up the slack when winter brought fewer visitors. Most of the year we had a pretty full house. A year and a half ago, we were returning from a routine doctor's visit for Sherrill. Calley and I went along just to get away and see a movie we both wanted to see. It was pouring rain and, right outside of town, a delivery truck swerved to avoid a mudslide on the highway and hit us head on."

Ginny gasped. "How horrible!"

He got up and walked to the screen, his voice fading back to her. "They were both killed outright—my wife and child. Calley was only seventeen years old, about to graduate from high school."

"Mr. Fredericks, I'm so sorry. I don't know what to say," Ginny said.

He turned back. "I had a compound fracture of both legs. You probably noticed my limp. One leg was much worse than the other. When I got out of the hospital, I sat in this house and didn't go out, didn't go to my therapy, didn't really care if I lived." He paused to gain control of his emotions. "I'm better, much better. I wake up now and thank God for what I had instead of blaming him for what was taken from me. But I still don't have the heart to start the business back."

"I can understand that," Ginny said, sympathetically.

He returned to the table. "I apologize for burdening you with my troubles. But it felt good to talk about it. I couldn't for so long. You're a very good listener. Thank you."

Ginny found it hard to chew. She had lost a sibling that she never knew she had. This man that she was supposed to hate seemed like a man in deep pain. How could she bring up what she had planned to say to him? He had suffered so much. Yet, she couldn't keep coming back up here. She had to have some closure in her own life, too.

"No, I'm glad you felt comfortable enough to tell me. I hope you don't think I was prying."

"No, not at all. Sometimes, when I do tell someone about it, it feels like a weight lifts, do you know what I mean?"

She smiled. "Yes, I do know what you mean. Something happened to me a long time ago; something that I just learned recently. It's been on my mind ever since. I'd like to tell you about it, if you don't mind."

He looked at her quizzically. "No, tell me anything you need to. Turn about is fair play, as they say. I've told you my story so you have the right to tell me yours."

"Well, for years I thought that my father was dead. That's what I was told as a child. But recently I found some old letters that led me to believe that he's alive. I talked to my mother about this, and she told me the real story. I had been lied to by my family. It seems that my father is alive, and through a friend, I was able to track him down." She paused, uncertain what to say next.

He rubbed his chin. "That's quite a story. Have you made contact with him yet?"

"Yes, I have," she said, her hand trembling as she removed her sunglasses and looked at him intently.

He frowned as he returned her stare. "Your eyes," he murmured, "are the same color as mine. Not a common color. Calley had gray-green eyes, too. And red hair."

"Like ours."

He smiled for a few seconds, then the smile faded as realization dawned on him, and he stammered,

"Wha…what are you saying? You think I'm…My daughter is dead. She was my only child." He rose, frowning in anger.

The sympathy she felt for him made her regret what she was about to say. But after weeks of conflicting emotions, the words tumbled out in a rush. "I lied to you, Mr. Fredericks. My name isn't Olivia Summers. It's Ginny Lee Cantrell. Do you remember your college days and a girl named Alison Cantrell?" She asked, boldly, even as her hands shook uncontrollably in her lap.

He sagged back down in his chair and gripped its arms, his face pale in the growing twilight.

Chapter 13

Neither said a word: John, because he was in shock, and Ginny, because she didn't know what to say next. The only noise was the whirring sound of the cicadas beyond the screened walls. Finally, he raised his head from his hands and looked at her.

"You're Alison's daughter?"

"I'm the product of your rape," she answered, pausing as she watched him flinch and drop his head again. "She and my grandmother always told me that you were dead, that you died in an accident. But I found some old letters and confronted my mother with them. I hated you when she told me the truth. But something made me want to find you, to let you know how much you hurt my mother. I wanted to find out why you left her without a word, to see just what kind of man you are."

He didn't speak, sitting with his head in his hands. She waited nervously for him to say something. Finally, he rubbed his eyes and got up to turn on the porch lights. She panicked, thinking he was walking out, wondering what she would do if he did. But he returned to the table and practically fell into his chair. He avoided looking into her eyes as he formed the words that were so difficult to say.

"Your mother told you what happened?" His voice was soft now, and he hesitated between words, reaching, searching. "I was so ashamed of myself," he began. "I couldn't believe my own behavior. Alison meant so much to me, and I ruined everything with that one stupid mistake. I was frantic after she left me. I called and called, but she wouldn't answer her phone, so I went to the dorm and got chased away by security. I walked back and forth from my dorm to hers most of the night, dodging authorities and hoping she would look out her window.

"When I couldn't find her the next day, I just got in my car like a crazy kid and headed out with little money and the clothes on my back. I stopped several times and tried to call, but got no answer. I wrote to her at her parents' after getting her address from the school, but she never replied. I kept on writing, hoping she would eventually answer. She was on my mind all the time. I had no idea that she was pregnant. I loved your mother, would have married her in a heartbeat if she could only forgive me.

"Believe me—you probably won't, but it's true anyway–I had never acted like that before with a girl. I was an angry young man, angry inside, angry with my parents. Maybe that's what made me act so horribly with your mother. I don't know." He shook his head.

"Anger at your parents is no excuse for…forcing someone," she retorted, her voice rising from its normally low pitch.

"You're right. I let things go too far. In spite of my youthful cockiness, I didn't know a lot about handling girls. Acting like a smart aleck got me by, covered up my ignorance. I can't tell you how much I hated myself, still do. If only I could have reached her, maybe she would have forgiven me, maybe even given me another chance."

"I doubt that," she snapped. "What happened after that? Where did you go?"

"I drove across country to my cousin's. He lived in Ventura, California, and I finally settled there. I held several jobs before getting on at one of the banks. I wrote to your mother many times during this time, but never received answers. It seemed as though she was through with me, and I didn't blame her. But I missed her—oh, I missed her." He choked and covered his mouth for a moment.

"My grandmother probably threw your letters away," Ginny interrupted. "She was a wonderful woman, but my mother confided to me that if you ever came back, Grammy would have pressed charges. My mother didn't want that. She was protective of you, even after what you put her through."

He almost smiled. "Then she might have answered if she'd known about my letters. That makes me feel a little bit better. I always thought she hated me." He cleared his throat and continued. "But you asked me about my life. I went to work at the bank and that's where I met

Sherrill. She was a sweet person, and we married after a short courtship. There seemed to be no hope of ever seeing your mother again. I was miserable and lonely, and Sherrill made a good home for us. I tried to be the best husband I could, and I think she was happy. I know she was when Calley was born and later when we moved here. She loved this house."

Ginny pushed back a strand of hair from her face, then asked, "Did you tell your wife about my mother and what you did?"

His voice, like low thunder, softened. "Yes, I did. When we decided to marry, I told her all about Alison and the guilt I felt. I wanted her to know all about me. She accepted me as I was. She knew that I had changed from the careless kid that I had been."

After a pause, Ginny rose. "Well, I don't know what else to ask. I first pictured you as a monster. Then my friend, who knows the story, convinced me that there might be another side. So I had to come and find out for myself. And you seem to be a decent person who made a bad mistake."

"This is such a shock. Ginny, is it? I can't believe…" he stammered, then continued, "Yes, I did an awful thing, I can't deny that. I've spent years with regret. But I'm glad to know that you had a normal childhood with people who loved you. I don't want to anger you any more than you are, but I wish I could have been a part of your life. Even if you do look like…me, you're a beautiful girl."

She stiffened and remained silent.

He grimaced. "I'm sorry, I shouldn't have said that. Is there anything I can do for you? I know I can't make up for my absence, but…"

She leaned forward, placed her hands on the table, and looked into his eyes. "As a matter of fact, there is. Come to my house and meet with my mother. Tell her that you tried to contact her, if that's really true. She had her life in gear before I found those letters and began asking questions. Now it's on her mind all over again. Give her some closure. Give us all closure."

His eyes brightened and the semblance of a smile appeared. "She knows you came here then?"

"No. I didn't tell her that I was searching for you. But I know that, after all these years, she's thought about you and wondered what happened to you. By the way, she never married, never really dated much."

He hung his head. "I ruined her life, didn't I? Except for having you. No, I can't. I can't surprise her like that. It wouldn't be fair. She wouldn't want to see me after all these years."

"Of course, I'd ask her before I tried to arrange a meeting. I wouldn't just throw this at her. But I'm almost sure she'd be agreeable, if only to clear up old wounds."

"No, I don't think so…I'd be too…" he murmured, his hands pressed to his face.

"Then there's nothing more to say. I'm glad I found you, and hope I haven't caused you any more pain. That wasn't my intention. I'll leave now." She walked across the porch and down the hall to her room. Her name echoed down the hall, but she felt too mentally exhausted to answer. Throwing her make-up back in her bag and grabbing up her purse, she opened her door. He was standing there looking helpless.

"Can't you stay longer? We really haven't cleared everything up. I know you have more you need to get off your chest about me, and I want to hear it, need to hear it. Please don't go. I didn't know you existed until an hour ago," he pleaded.

She set her bag down. "I think we've said it all for now. If you want to talk more, you'll have to come to me." She fished in her purse for her card and handed it to him. He stared at the card, and then reached out for her hand. She hesitated, but briefly laid her hand in his.

"I'm glad you came, but I wish you'd stay just one more day. I haven't learned anything about you," he begged.

She wanted desperately to respond to the plea in his voice. But she was afraid that she might be drawn in by his deep voice and forget what her mother went through because of him. It wouldn't be fair. And soon she had to face Alison with what she had done.

Picking up her bag, she walked to her car without looking back.

Chapter 14

Ginny began the long drive home reliving every word, every moment at Calley's Cottage as she maneuvered down the dark winding roads. She could still see John reaching for her hand, the plea in his eyes for her to stay. Why did she leave so abruptly? To hurt him? Possibly. But she wanted to leave the ball in his court. She had done all she could without telling her mother about it. As she imagined telling Allison what she had done, she ran off the road and overcorrected, forcing her attention back to her driving. Her brain was already on overload, so she put that particular thought out of her mind.

Midway, she stopped for coffee and called Noah. Martha answered.

"Hi, Ginny. No, Noah hasn't come back from the gym. He and his friend, Carl, probably went for a bite after workout. They sometimes do that. How are you, dear?"

"I'm fine. Tell Noah that I'm on my way home. Should be there in a couple of hours."

"I'll tell him. And you be careful, hear?"

Having been denied the comfort of his voice, she began to sob. Sitting under the neon lights of the drive-in restaurant, she let the tears flow unchecked. Feeling better after a good cry, she made the rest of the drive in record time, but found herself wondering why he didn't call her back on her cell phone. Desperate to get back to her own safe haven, she gave a sigh of relief as she turned onto the dark, familiar street.

But her relief was short lived. There was a patrol car in front of the house.

The porch light was on, and Noah was sitting in the swing. He jumped up and was at her car door when she stopped the car, pulling her into a tight hug.

She pushed back, visions of disasters running through her head. "Something's happened. Is it Mom? Grace?"

"No, honey, nothing like that. Some kids broke into your house tonight. They came in through the kitchen window."

"What?" She stared in disbelief. At that moment, a policeman stepped out onto the porch.

Noah introduced her to the officer. "Miss Cantrell, I'm not sure if anything was taken. We need you to come in and go through the house. Noah here scared the kids off, and he thinks that they didn't have time to take much." He nodded at Noah.

"You scared them off? What happened?" She leaned against Noah's shoulder, still shaking.

He tightened his arm around her. "Must have been about an hour ago. I was about to call you when I heard Grover barking and looked out the window. Then I heard him yelp, like he was hurt, so I came over to see. He was on your porch, bleeding. Then I heard footsteps running out the back. I ran after them, but they cut through Grace's yard, and I lost them in the dark."

"He called 911, and we caught two of them on Center Street, hiding in some bushes," Officer Pullman finished. "They were just kids. I'm guessing this was done on a dare from the way they talked. One of the boys said that yesterday they had seen you put bags in your car and drive off so they knew that you were gone."

Ginny shook her head in disbelief. "Where are they?"

"They're at the station. You'll need to come down and press charges later."

Ginny and Noah went through the house. The boys had knocked over a table in their haste to leave. Smashed glass from a picture frames and vase littered the hall. The kitchen floor was crunchy with glass slivers from the broken window, but Noah had already nailed a board over it. Black fingerprint dust had sifted over the sink and countertop.

Ginny checked her jewelry. Laura Belle's pearls and diamond ring were still in their box. A quick walk through the house showed everything else was in its place. Even so, she shuddered at the violation of her space.

"I don't believe they took anything," she said to the officer.

"Good," he said. "There was nothing on the two we caught, but so far they haven't told us who their accomplice was. Just wanted to be sure he didn't make off with anything. Those kids are only thirteen years old. They've never been in trouble before."

"What about their parents?" she asked.

"We've contacted them. From what they told the officer, they were willing to let them stay in jail for awhile. I think they'd like to teach them a lesson."

"So would I. Why don't I just wait a day or two before I do anything? Could I do that?"

"Well, a few hours won't hurt," he grinned. "If you'll come down to the station in the morning, we'll do what we need to."

Ginny thanked him, and he pulled off in his cruiser. Turning to Noah, she sighed. "I don't know if I'll ever feel safe again. I'm sure glad you saw them before they found Grammy's jewelry or made a bigger mess."

"Grover sounded the alarm."

"Oh, Grover. I forgot about him. You said he was bleeding. Where is he?"

"I called Dr. Wilson; he was the nearest vet. He picked him up and took him to his office. I don't think Grover's badly hurt."

"Take me over there. I want to be sure he's okay."

They got in her car and drove a few streets over to the vet's. Dr. Wilson was still there and took them to the back where the dog lay in a cage surrounded by disturbed tenants, all barking and mewing in confusion. Grover's bushy tail twirled in circles when he saw them.

"You caught me about to leave," Dr. Wilson said as he let Grover out of the cage. "This fellow's fine, except for a few stitches behind his ear," He showed them the wound, neatly stitched on shaved skin. "They must have hit him with something fairly sharp or maybe kicked him with a sharp heel. He's going to be okay, and he's definitely ready to go home."

Ginny smiled at the dog that obviously was still under the influence of the local anesthetic and not in any pain. "He doesn't belong to either of us, but I'll gladly take him back to the owners down the street."

"There's a problem there, Ginny," Noah said. "Didn't Grover belong to the people in the gray shingled house?"

"I think so. I met them once when I first moved back. They were renters, I think. Why?"

"Well, yesterday a moving van was there, and I noticed coming home from work today that the house looks empty."

"You mean they just left Grover?" She bent, putting her forehead against the yellow furred head and smelled the antiseptic on his wound. "How could they just move off and leave this sweet dog?"

"I don't understand that either. Maybe they thought he would be okay since everybody on the street seemed to look after him. You once said you'd like to have one just like him. Looks like you got your wish."

Dr. Wilson cleared his throat, and they realized they were keeping him. So Noah paid the bill, and they set off with Grover in the back seat, panting and wriggling.

Ginny groaned. "What a day! What a night! I've gained a parent…and a dog. Well, I'm glad to have Grover with me. He'll make me feel safer, I hope."

He pulled her car into the garage. "Let's go in and clean up the glass. Then I want to sit down and hear about your trip," he said, as he got out of the car, stretching his tall frame and yawning.

"It's so late, Noah. I'm not sure I have the energy left to go into it tonight. The glass can wait until morning."

"I'm good for an hour or so, but if that's what you want." He took her hands. "You look so tired. Are you sure you don't want to sleep over at our house? You were pretty shook up."

"I'll be okay. I'll keep Grover in my room. He'll be my guard dog." She patted the warm head. "Thank you so much, Noah."

"Call me at the paper when you wake up, okay?"

"Okay," she murmured with a yawn. She had never felt such mental and physical exhaustion.

"I'll go in a little early so we can have breakfast together. Now you take Grover in and get to bed. I'm happy that you're home safely, but I'm glad you weren't here when those kids broke in." He kissed her, and she held on to him for a long time before she took the dog's leash and went in, locking the door behind her.

Grover was delighted to come inside. She found an old blanket and made him a bed right beside hers. After sniffing everything in the room, he sank right down on the blanket. He seemed as beat as she was. She left the lights on in the hall to ease her anxiety over the break-in and threw herself on the bed fully clothed. In spite of all the drama of the evening, she was asleep immediately.

The next sound she heard was Grover's bark as the doorbell rang, and she sprang straight up in bed. It took a few seconds to come out of her fog and remember that Grover was now her roommate. Following him to the door, she found Noah standing there with a bag of donuts and two large coffees.

"Great! You get to see me first thing in the morning. That should chase you away," she teased as she ran her fingers through her tangled hair. Looking down at her wrinkled slacks and blouse, she added, "but at least I'm dressed. Shouldn't we go to the station and get those boys charged and released now?"

"Later. Right now I want you to sit and drink your coffee!" He ordered. "I'm putting Grover out back. Got anything to feed him?"

She frowned. "No, but there's some old bread...well, here I'll help you." They rounded up bread and water for Grover who lapped it up before he began his tour of the fenced back yard.

Back in the living room, they settled down with their impromptu breakfast, and Ginny finally got to tell Noah all the details of her trip and the meeting with her father.

When she had finished, he asked, "When are you going to tell your mother about this?"

Ginny pushed the hair back off her face and sighed. "This weekend. She's coming this weekend. I just hope she isn't too upset with me."

Noah pulled her into his arms. "She won't blame you for trying to find your father. You couldn't have a more understanding mother. She loves you. And Ginny," he murmured into her hair, "I love you, too"

She turned and looked into his dark eyes. "Noah, darling. You're the best thing that has ever happened to me."

"And…" he coaxed.

"And…I love you, too."

Chapter 15

"Hey Mom, you're early," Ginny greeted Alison the next afternoon. "I didn't expect you until tomorrow afternoon."

"I took today off and decided to come on so we could have a few more hours together. Hope its okay. I'm glad you're not out with the door locked because I left my key on my other ring. Don't know why I picked up my spare…Well, who is this?" she remarked, looking down at Grover as he leaned against her legs with his tail awhirl.

"Do you remember Grover? No? He used to wander the neighborhood. Anyway, his owners moved and left him so now he's mine." She smiled proudly at the new family member. "He tried to protect the house against those burglars, didn't you, boy?"

"Burglars? What do you mean 'burglars'? Were you in the house? Did they take anything?" Alison asked in alarm.

"No, relax. Give me your bag and come on in. I'll tell you the whole story."

With Alison's belongings deposited in her old bedroom, they went to the kitchen and poured glasses of iced tea. Ginny was grateful that Noah had replaced the window glass before her mother arrived. Taking their tea to the back porch, they settled in the comfortable old wicker. The whir of the neighborhood air conditioners testified to the heat and humidity of the morning.

"We won't sit here long," Ginny said as she turned on the ceiling fan. "This is supposed to be one of the hottest days of the year."

"Right now, it's fine," Alison said, as she settled with her feet curled under her on the settee. "Now tell me about your excitement with the robbers." She pushed back her dark hair and waited for Ginny to answer. At that moment, Ginny was thinking that her mother was one of the most beautiful women she knew. In shorts and a tee shirt, she looked more like an older sister.

Ginny told her the story of the break-in, carefully omitting where she was returning from at the time. She finished with, "...so Noah and Grover saved the day!"

"And how is Noah?" Alison smiled and cocked her head.

"He's wonderful. Oh, Mom. I'm really in love. He's the neatest person, so kind and considerate."

Alison closed her eyes and nodded. "I hope you aren't rushing things, Ginny. You haven't known him very long."

Ginny knew that she was remembering her own brief romance with John. "No, Mom. We aren't rushing.

We're still getting to know each other. But we're both pretty sure that this is it."

Alison reached across and squeezed her daughter's hand. "Then I'm happy for you. You know I always wanted you to have the best."

"He is the best, Mom."

"Hello. Got any of that tea for me?" Grace called as she stuck her head around the screened door. She gave Alison a quick squeeze and collapsed in the opposite chair. "I've been making pickles, and my feet and back feel like they are about to break."

While Ginny went in to fix Grace's tea, Alison settled back in the settee and spoke softly to her oldest friend. "Well, Grace, she tells me she's in love."

"Yep. I knew it was a match from day one. And I betcha there's a wedding before long."

"Please, Grace," Alison groaned. "Not so fast. Do you really think he's right for Ginny?"

"Well, isn't that obvious?" Grace snorted. "She couldn't do any better than Noah."

Ginny returned with the tea, and the three women sat and chatted. A cooling breeze began to stir, announcing that a rain would soon be blowing up. Ginny was half-listening to Grace's conversation about town politics. She was thinking that this might be a good time to tell both women about her trip to meet her father. But just as she found a good opening, it began to sprinkle, and Grace left to return to her pickle making, running through the yard like a kid.

"I hope she stays this healthy and active," Alison remarked as she fondly watched the older woman disappear into her house. "I don't know what we'd ever do without her."

The rain accompanied with thunder drove them inside where Ginny showed her mother the changes that she had made to the house since Alison was last there. She was amazed at how much Ginny had done.

"It looks wonderful. I didn't realize you were turning into such a decorator. Your grandmother would be so pleased. She would love the changes you've made." Alison admired the deep green paint and the wallpaper that Ginny had added to the dining room.

The day passed with grocery shopping, cooking, and short naps, and still Ginny hadn't told her mother about the trip. Every time she found an opening, the phone rang or there was an interruption of some kind. The more time passed, the more nervous she became. Finally Alison noticed that Ginny couldn't keep her mind on their conversations.

"Honey, you seem awfully jittery. Is this what love does for you?"

She shook her head, a frown creasing her brow. "I've done something, Mom, and I need to tell you. But I don't know how to start."

Alison plopped down on the sofa and patted the pillow beside her. "Well, sit down and get on with it. Just what have you done now, Ginny Lee?"

Ginny sat next to her mother, took a deep breath, and began. As she listened to the first details, Alison's mouth dropped open. Her face grew red as she started to protest, but Ginny held up her hand. By the time the story unfolded, Alison had twisted her shirttail into a knot. Silence fell over the room. Ginny waited anxiously for her mother to comment.

Finally Alison smoothed down her shirt and sighed. "I can't believe that you did this without saying a word to me first. I can understand you wanting to meet your father, but you could have prepared me for it. This comes as a shock. I never really expected you to go looking for him. Not after all that I told you."

Ginny touched her mother's shoulder. "I knew you wouldn't want me to do it, Mom. But I needed to know what he was like, to see the person who fathered me. I wouldn't have had to do this if you'd been honest with me from the start."

With tears in her eyes, Alison dropped her head and nodded. "You're right. I'll always regret that." She rose and walked around the room with her arms folded. After a long pause, she turned back to Ginny and asked in her soft gentle voice, "How did he look?"

"He's turning a little gray at the temples and has a bit of a limp from his injuries in the accident. Since I hadn't seen him before, I really don't know how he's changed in looks. He seemed a little depressed—I guess he would after all he's been through. I was cruel in some of the things I said, but he had it coming. At the end, I told him that if there was to be any more communication between us, he'd have to come here to see me. He begged me to stay a little longer, but I just walked away."

Alison sat back down, put her arm around her daughter, and pulled her curly red head against her dark one. "My poor baby. You felt like you have to seek revenge for me, didn't you?"

"Sure I did. But I believe him, Mom, when he said he tried to contact you over and over. I don't think he made that up."

"No, he probably didn't. I knew about a few times when he tried to talk to me on the phone, but your grandmother told him to leave us alone. At the time, I thought she knew best. Now I realize I should have been allowed to handle the situation myself. But that's all in the past. Can't go back and change things now."

"Mom, did you forgive him?"

"I put it out of my mind—blame, forgiveness didn't register with me. I had you to bring up and remembering hurt too much. I just concentrated on the present and the joy of raising you."

Ginny took her mother's face in her hands. "You're a brave woman, Alison Cantrell, and I'm proud to have you for a mother."

Alison blinked back a tear, then laughed as the click of Grover's nails on the wood floor broke the tension. The big yellow dog danced at their feet, tail awhirl. "Here's our hero," she said as he jumped up and wiggled between them on the sofa. They hugged and petted Grover who rewarded them with a doggy smile on his broad face.

No more was said until after dinner. As they sipped coffee in the dining room, content after a dinner of salmon and salad, Alison looked at Ginny with a smile.

"You know, I'm not sorry you found your father. Maybe it would be a good idea if we met sometime, now that everything is out in the open. It might help me, too…might let me get rid of old hurts that are still buried in here somewhere." She patted her chest.

Ginny almost dropped her cup. "Are you sure, Mom?"

"Yeah, I'm sure. Do you think we could drive up some weekend?"

"If he wants to see us, he'll have to come here. That's the way I left it. I can call and ask him to drive down, if you really want me to. But I don't feel like we should go to him."

Alison nodded silently and carried their cups to the kitchen. She didn't know then, but she wouldn't have long to wait to see John again. The next morning, just before noon, there was a knock on the door.

Chapter 16

When she opened the door, Ginny's smile faded to a look of shock. She hardly recognized John with his fresh haircut and neat khakis and yellow sport shirt. He smiled nervously and shifted from foot to foot as he spoke. "Ginny, I know I should have called first. But you said that I would have to come to you, and here I am, praying that you might give me a little of your time. I hope you're not angry."

"What…what if I had been gone?" She stammered.

"Then I would have waited," he replied in a soft but firm tone. "I apologize for showing up out of the blue, but after you left I got so excited about our meeting, and I just had to see you. If it's a bad time, I can come back, just say…"

She motioned for him to come in, and he smiled his thanks as she closed the stained glass door and leaned against it. "My mother is here," she said simply.

He froze. "Then it's not a good time, is it? She might not want me here."

"She knows that I came to see you. It's okay. I told her all about it," she assured him as she led him to the living room. "Just let me go tell her so she won't be shocked. She's in the back yard, watering plants. Sit down and I'll be right back."

He lowered himself slowly to the sofa and watched his daughter walk away. He thought she was even lovelier in cut off shorts and a faded baggy shirt than when she had been in Calley's Cottage. He heard her call "Mom", and his heart was in his throat. He needed to come here so badly, but he hadn't really expected to see Alison. What would he say to her? And what would Alison say to him? Whatever she said would be what he deserved, but still anxiety flooded his whole body.

He stood when the two women came into the room, Alison slightly behind Ginny. She looked a little older, but just as beautiful with her dark eyes and hair. His knees felt like jelly, and he could hardly get his breath.

"Hello, Alison," he said in a ragged voice.

"John. This is a surprise. I didn't ever expect to see you again."

"You…probably hoped you'd never lay eyes on me, here or anywhere else. I hope you aren't mad at Ginny for this."

Alison took the chair across from him. "No, John. I could never be angry with my…with Ginny. She's the one who has suffered the most from this unexpected discovery."

"You're right, of course. You look well, Alison."

"You, too. Ginny told me about her visit and also about the loss of your wife and daughter. I'm very sorry."

He leaned forward, struggling to keep his voice even. "Thank you. I didn't expect sympathy from you. I'm the one who should be apologizing after all the trouble I caused you. I'm a different man than the one you knew, Alison. It won't make up for my mistakes, but maybe you'll see me in a little better light. I wish things had been different."

"So do I, John. But since you're here, we might as well clear the air. I have a lot to say to you, things that have been on my mind for years." Alison held her shaking hands, felt her heart pounding with tension.

He nodded. "I'm ready to hear whatever you have to say to me. Lord knows, I deserve it. You couldn't say anything that I haven't already said to myself."

Ginny watched the two of them, so uncomfortable with each other. Funny, but she felt at ease with her father in spite of his past history. She had to remind herself that her mother had good reason to feel anxious. After a long silence when neither seemed to know how to start, she made a suggestion.

"Why don't I leave the two of you alone? I'm sure you would be more comfortable if I weren't here." She rose to leave. "Mom, I'm going to Grace's unless you want me to stay."

Alison hesitated, and then agreed. Ginny called to Grover, who had come in from his napping spot by her bed, and they went out the back. Crossing the yard, she knocked at Grace's door.

"Why are you knocking, honey? Just come on in," Grace called from the kitchen table where she was having a sandwich. "Want me to fix you one?" she offered as Ginny sat down at the table.

"No, thanks. Can I sit with you while my parents have a long overdue conversation?"

Grace choked on a mouthful of toasted pimento cheese. "Your WHO? What on earth are you talking about?"

"John is here. He showed up on the doorstep not knowing if I'd be at home and certainly not knowing Mom would be here."

Grace took a big gulp of water. "Oh, my goodness, I can't believe this is happening. Are you sure your mother will be okay?"

"She said she wanted to see him. We just didn't expect it to be today."

"That scoundrel! I'm amazed that she'd agree to see him at all after all these years."

"Grace, I need to tell you why John is here." She accepted a glass of water and told her dumbfounded neighbor about her trip to Laurel Springs and her encounter with John. Grace's eyes were wide with amazement.

"Ginny, Ginny," she exclaimed. "You may have caused more trouble than you know. But I understand, honey, why you wanted to find him. I really do." She patted the red head, as though Ginny were still a child. "So that's why you didn't want me to go to Laurel Springs with you."

"I hated lying to you, Grace. But I simply had to go, to find out about him."

An hour went by, and Ginny and Grace were both getting antsy wondering what was being said at the house next door. Finally, Grace put down her embroidery. "I'm going over there. I'd like to tell him a thing or two myself, even if it's not my business."

"Now, now, Grace. Mom can handle herself. She'll..." Her voice trailed off as she saw her mother coming across the yard. "Here she comes."

Alison followed their voices to the den. She looked flushed and nervous.

"You okay, Mom?" Ginny asked anxiously.

"I'm fine, honey. Just wanted to tell you that John and I are going to lunch. He hasn't eaten a bite today, and I think we'll be more comfortable in another setting where there are people milling about. It's so quiet in the house and it makes us feel even more self conscious."

"You're going to LUNCH WITH HIM?" Grace blurted out.

"We have a lot to discuss, Grace. Please don't worry. See you both later." She turned abruptly and left, leaving Grace with her mouth agape.

It was mid-afternoon when they returned. Ginny and Noah were in the kitchen; Ginny was trying to concentrate on putting together a pie as Noah called out the recipe. Hearing the door close, Ginny wiped her hands and rushed into the living room. But John and Alison were still standing in the hall, talking in low voices. She was showing him the pictures hanging there of Ginny at various ages. He was smiling and asking questions, Alison patiently answering. Ginny wanted to linger and listen, but instead she motioned Noah back into the kitchen, and they finished the pie. As she slid the cobbler into the oven, John and Alison entered the kitchen.

"Hello, Noah. I believe you know who this is. John Fredericks, Noah Johnstone." Alison watched as the two men shook hands, John slightly smaller than Noah.

"Thank you, Noah," John said as he released his hand. "I heard that you're the friend that found me on the Internet. I'm so grateful that you did that." The usually articulate Noah just nodded and smiled.

"Was lunch okay?" Ginny asked her mother nervously.

"It was fine. We ate at the diner, noisy but good comfort food." She patted her daughter's arm. "Don't be worried. We were able to clear the air about a lot of things." Alison gave John a slight smile.

Ginny suddenly felt very awkward and busied herself making lemonade from scratch rather that the mix she usually used. Noah stayed in the kitchen with her while John and Alison went into the living room.

"Well, what do you think?" Noah finally asked the silent Ginny.

"They seemed to be more at ease with each other now. And Noah, darling, they wouldn't be talking at all if you hadn't found him for me." She put her arms around him and nestled her face in his neck, inhaling the scent of soap and fabric softener.

"But you seem apprehensive," he said, pulling back to look into her face.

"I am, I guess. I never really expected them to have this much to say to each other. My mother never had closure with John, and I suppose that takes time to work out."

"What about you? Do you feel better than you did before you found him—or worse?"

"Oh, better. Much better. You know, Noah, I can't dislike the man. I think he's dealing with so much grief—and regret, too, since he found out about me. There was such a void in his life when his family was killed. Maybe this has given him something else to think about, the fact that he has another daughter."

He rocked her in his arms. "I'm not sure that I could be as forgiving as you and your mother. But I'm glad you're that way because you won't stay mad at me when we have our fights."

She pulled away and grinned at him. "Are we going to have fights?"

"Probably. But lots of making up, too." He was kissing her when Alison called that John was leaving. He was standing by the front door.

"Just wanted to say goodbye, Ginny. Thank you for finding me, for your visit, for everything. It's changed my life just knowing about you." He looked as though he might choke up and Ginny found tears in her own eyes.

"Are...are you coming back?" She asked.

"Unless you want me to stay away, I'll be back often. Next time I'll call first, though. Don't want to make a nuisance of myself," he laughed shakily as he gave her hand a quick kiss, and was out the door, Alison walking quietly beside him to his car.

"Well! This is just too weird." Ginny murmured. But she had a broad smile on her face.

Chapter 17

That night, Alison told Ginny most of what had transpired between her and John. She recalled that she had vented all the anger that had remained through the years. John had patiently agreed that it was well deserved, but also told her about the letters and calls and all the times that he had tried to make contact but was discouraged by Alison's parents. He had apologized over and over for his actions. And though she didn't tell Ginny, she realized more and more that she had played a big part in what happened. Agreeing that they were both very inexperienced in dealing with the opposite sex, they parted on a friendlier basis that either of them expected.

"So do you think you'll see John again?" Ginny asked.

Alison quickly answered, "No. No, there's no reason for us to see each other again, unless it's for your wedding or the birth of grandchildren, or something like that." She winked at Ginny and said good night.

Ginny let Grover out the back door, and he lingered, sniffing every tree and shrub, until she impatiently called him in. Settled in her bed, she tried to read, but soon lost interest. Something like disappointment prickled at her insides. How she had expected the day to go, she wasn't sure. Maybe in the back of her mind, she wanted her parents to forget the past and find each other again, falling into each other's arms. How foolish and romantic she was.

"I'm worse than Grace," she grumbled as she turned out the light.

Alison stayed for church and lunch, and then changed into jeans for the drive home. Ginny waited for her mother to say more about yesterday's events, but she remained silent on the subject, and Ginny didn't press it.

Although her father's visit crossed her mind occasionally, Ginny didn't have a lot of time to dwell on anything the next two weeks. She took supplies to her new schoolroom and put up crisp up-to date alphabet pictures around the top of the room to replace the frayed ones that had been there for years. She set up her reading corner and brought goldfish for her students to enjoy. The first week was spent in meeting and getting acquainted with the other teachers. The principal, Mr. Aldridge, was a classmate friend of her mother's, and he had known Ginny since childhood.

Then the first day of school arrived, hot and humid. She loved the first day, getting to know her first graders. Some were shy, being firmly pushed ahead by mothers, some with a younger sibling in tow. One little boy cried so when his mother left that Ginny had to quickly interest him in a computer game before separation anxiety struck all over the classroom. But most were eager, examining the books and decorations, the fish and Grover, who was allowed to come for the short first day. All were innocent minds ready to be molded. Ginny was in her element, moving among them, making them feel comfortable. She knew how to gain their respect, but, at the same time, could make learning fun. Hugs would be a regular part of the day soon.

Busy with her job and seeing Noah often, her life was so full that she only thought of John when he called, and he did so every week to see how things were going for her. She talked to her mother at least twice a week, and Alison seemed glad that Ginny and John were becoming friends. But she didn't speak of John unless Ginny mentioned him.

The only blot on Ginny's happiness was Martha Johnstone's illness. She was becoming weaker every day, and Noah spent more and more time with her. The pain that hadn't been a big problem before was now with her most of the time. Noah had a nurse with her while he worked, and Ginny often sat with her when she got out of school. Martha's bravery was touching; she didn't complain. But it was taking more and more pain medication to keep her moderately comfortable.

After settling Martha in bed for the night, Ginny and Noah sat on his front porch. An earlier thunderstorm brought the first chill of mid September. Wet red leaves littered the floor beneath their feet as they drifted back and forth in the swing.

"I wish she could make it until Christmas," Noah said as he laid his head back against the swing.

"But do you want her to if she's suffering even more?" Ginny held his hand to her cheek.

"No, she's suffered more than enough already. I just thought we would have one more holiday together."

"And you might," Ginny said, knowing that it wasn't a probability. Pulling the old afghan tighter, Ginny leaned against him. "This is so difficult for you, too. But you've been the best son. You've taken such good care of your mother, and she loves you for it. When the end comes, you can take some comfort from that."

He pounded the swing with his fist and cried out with a trembling voice. "She's a good woman, a good mother. She's only fifty-one, too young to go like this." With that he broke down, and Ginny held him while the damp wind swirled around them, the very air heavy with mourning.

Martha's family was at her house most of the time, and Ginny and Noah saw little of each other. Ginny helped as much as she could without intruding on the family time.

A month later, having refused to go to the hospital, Martha lapsed into unconsciousness, much to Noah's relief, since the pain had grown unbearable. During the three days before her death, Grace and Ginny, when she could, manned the coffeepot and kept food coming to Noah and his uncle and the various cousins who lived nearby. During this time, Ginny saw another side of

Noah. He was stoic and quietly spent time with the other family members offering comfort to them. But Ginny knew his pain, being an only child herself. She couldn't imagine how she would get through the loss of her own mother.

Martha was buried on a bright October day. All were relieved that it wasn't raining, as it had been the day before. The brilliant maple leaves still clung to the trees, fiery reds and yellows against an azure sky.

"Mom loved this time of year. October was her favorite month. She loved the change in temperature, the leaves falling." Noah said, as they walked away from the grave long after friends and other family had gone. Ginny clung to his arm as they strolled through the fallen leaves.

"And now she's no longer in pain," she murmured as they reached the funeral director's sedan. They rode in silence back to the chapel. As Noah slid into his car, Ginny leaned across and said, "After the lunch with the family, I want you to go to bed. You're completely exhausted, darling."

He nodded absently, his mind far away to a time when his mother was young and healthy. He could see her helping him with his pitching when he went out for the baseball team, her bright eyes as she brought in his homemade birthday cakes every year, waiting up for him when he was out with the guys. He smiled for a moment when he remembered catching his mother and father in a wild embrace on the sofa, and her blush as she pulled herself back together. He could almost feel her hands on each side of his face, lovingly caressing away his bad days or his broken heart. Tears squeezed between his lids, and he rested his head on the back of the seat and let them flow unchecked.

Later, when the entire crowd left the house, Ginny and Grace sent him to bed, and he didn't protest. They cleaned the kitchen and slipped out, closing all the blinds and taking the phone off the hook.

Ginny left him a note.

My darling. I'm here if you need me. You need to catch up on your sleep. The leftover food is in the fridge and everything is marked. Come over when you feel ready. I'll be right here. All my love.

Chapter 18

Alison was in a nervous tizzy. Clothes were strewn all over her bed, tried on and discarded. She added a purple pantsuit to the pile after woefully discovering that the pants were too tight and the jacket wouldn't button. Sighing, she sat down in the middle of the scattered apparel. There was no time to go shopping for a new outfit. She would have to pull the first dress from the bottom of the pile and press it. The bright blue at least brought out her dark skin, even if it was several years old.

She ran both hands through her mussed hair. Why had she agreed to see John again? She had told herself, should he ever ask, she would say no. There was just no reason whatsoever to see him again. They had worked out their feelings, for the most part, and that's the way it should be left. But when he called and said he would like to drive down and take her to dinner, she agreed with no hesitation.

"What's the matter with me?" she asked Monroe, the striped tabby that watched her every move from atop the stack of decorative pillows on her bed. He purred at the sound of her voice and blinked his big yellow eyes. "Crazy, you say?" She picked him up, batting at the loose cat hair in his wake, and held him close. Monroe almost groaned when she scratched him behind his ears, and struggled to knead himself a comfy place in her lap. But she put him down, noting that she had exactly thirty minutes to dress and put on her make-up. He walked away, stiff legged, showing his contempt for her tease.

Just as she finished her eye make-up, the doorbell rang. "Oh, no," she murmured as she tossed on her robe. John stood awkwardly in the doorway holding a bouquet of flowers.

"I'm a little early," he said, apologetically. "Want me to drive around for awhile?"

"That's okay," she pulled her robe tightly around her and accepted the flowers. "These are beautiful, thank you so much. I'll go put them in a vase. Make yourself comfortable. Can I get you something?"

"I'm fine." Watching her disappear into her tiny kitchen for the vase, he backed up to a chair and started to sit.

Monroe let out a yowl that brought John back to his feet quickly. Alison looked around the kitchen door. "You've just met Monroe. I live here with him," she said, laughing at the indignant cat with raised back that skittered sideways to hide behind another chair. "Don't mind him; he's a little picky about who comes around. He's my guard cat."

By the time she finished dressing, she found Monroe on John's lap, purring contentedly while having his ears scratched.

"Traitor," she hissed at the cat, as John released him and rose to help her on with her coat.

Since it was a chilly, rainy, weekday evening, the restaurant was only half full. Their table was by the window but still close to the fireplace, and the heat felt good.

"What wine do you prefer?" John asked.

"I don't drink, but you order whenever you'd like," she insisted. "I'd really love a cup of hot tea."

"I remember. You never drank in college. And neither do I." He turned to the waiter and ordered their meal of blackened salmon with immediate cups of tea. The conversation was strained at first, both trying too hard to make small talk. Then Alison told John about Martha Johnstone's death that week.

"I'm sorry to hear that," he said. "Noah seems like such a nice young man."

"He is. And Ginny loves him. I wouldn't be surprised if they become engaged."

"Really! She hasn't mentioned that to me in our phone conversations. Mostly she talked about school and the things her students did. She really loves teaching, doesn't she?"

They dove into their salads, then the fish that was cooked to perfection. The restaurant had filled up, and as they ate, they made a game of guessing what the people in the neighboring tables did for a living. As they laughed and relaxed more, they noted that the couples on each side of them talked on their cell phones at one time or another during their meal.

"People carry those things everywhere." Alison marveled. "I only take mine along for emergency or to check in with Ginny when I'm on the road."

"You notice mine is back in my car. I certainly don't feel the need to use it while I'm having dinner. We're hopelessly out of date, I guess," he observed with a grin.

Later, over their last cup of tea, they became thoughtful, watching the rain coming down in sheets, blurring the vista, making the restaurant seem like its own little world. John finally felt relaxed enough to be quiet and observe Alison. She didn't look much different, still beautiful, just a little heavier but that was becoming to her. She still had that bright smile, even after all that had transpired between them.

"The years have been very kind to you," he said. "You're as lovely as you were when you were in college."

She stiffened for a moment, and then exhaled. "Thank you. I've had it fairly easy, living at home until I moved away and took this job after Ginny went to college. I had no husband to tie me down. I could always go back home if I so chose. And still could. Ginny would let me move back in with her in a minute. But I like my job, and I'm basically content in my little place with my cat. Sounds like an old maid, doesn't it?"

"You had it rough raising Ginny, I'm sure, even with your mother's help. And the last ten years, I've only been an hour's drive from you. I wish I'd known about Ginny."

She nodded. "I wish I had told you. But that was then and this is now. We can't change the past, John." She paused and glanced out the window. "Shall we leave while the rain has slacked up?" He paid the bill and reluctantly helped her on with her coat, feeling like he caused the evening to end too soon by bringing up past history. But when they got back to her apartment, she asked him in for caramel pie, and he accepted with a relieved smile. They spent two more hours talking in Alison's cozy little kitchen with the sound of the rain pouring onto the tin roofed stoop outside. She told him more stories of Ginny's childhood. John loosened up and told her more about Calley, the daughter he lost.

It grew late, and he noticed that she stifled a yawn. "You're tired. I'd better go," he said, rising stiffly on his injured leg.

"John, I've enjoyed the dinner and our talks. Thank you for coming down and for the lovely flowers." She handed him his jacket, and he put it on slowly. Then turning to her, he held out his hand to hers.

"Alison, this has been great. I didn't believe that you'd accept my invitation. I can't tell you what it meant to me. Would I be…too out of line if I ask you to go out with me again? I mean, could we start over as mature adults and see where it leads?"

She felt the flush run from the top of her head to her toes. "John, we had a pleasant evening. Let's let it go at that. We'll see each other from time to time at Ginny's, I'm sure."

"No," he replied, "I don't want to see you only at Ginny's. I know it's a reach for you to see me on a regular basis, but at least think about having dinner with me occasionally. I feel like we've become friends again. Isn't that a good place to start?"

She saw the pleading in his eyes. Her heart was beating so hard she felt sure that he could hear it.

"I'll think about it, John. Give me a little time."

"Take all the time you want. I'll be right down the road. Good night." He took both hands and squeezed them hard, smiling as he closed the door behind him.

She dropped into a chair feeling strangely disjointed, like a bowl of Jell-O. Monroe wove sleepily from the sofa to her chair and sat down in front of her, his eyes heavy.

She looked down at him, shaking her head. "Monroe, we can't tell Ginny about this. She would get all caught up in it. And it can't go anywhere. There's just too much history between us. I'm crazy to have allowed tonight to happen." Monroe yawned and led the way to the bedroom. It was way past his bedtime, and he was bored with the whole thing.

Chapter 19

The last school bus pulled away, and Ginny, having had bus duty all week, gratefully turned away and walked back to her room.

"Have a good weekend," a fellow teacher called.

"You, too."

Ginny gathered up her things, very happy that it was Friday afternoon. It had been a good week, but she was tired. She hadn't caught up with her rest since the week before when Martha passed away and was buried.

Noah had been busy taking care of the legalities after the funeral. Before he could get his bearings again, the paper sent him out of town on a story, so he wouldn't be home until Monday. She would miss him this weekend, but thought that even as tired as he was, a change of scene would do him good.

She took the long way home, past the City Park where the leaves were the most colorful. Varieties of oaks, maples, dogwoods, and birches flaunted their brightest colors yet, spectacular against the vivid blue sky. Unable to resist, she pulled over and found a park bench to sit for awhile. Skateboarders whizzed past her; mother's with babies in their strollers passed by. All seemed to be rushing to soak up the warmth before the winds and rains of late fall blew the leaves in sodden masses to the ground.

Her thoughts turned to the mountains. How beautiful it must be up there right now. She had a sudden urge to drive up for the weekend. The longer she considered it, the more excited she became. She felt like John would be glad to see her, and she could take some books and have a good rest. Shot through with energy at the thought, she impulsively called him on her cell phone.

John answered the phone, sounding very pleased that she was coming. She hurried home, threw a few things into a bag, and checked in with Grace, who was not at all pleased.

"Ginny, do you think this is a good idea? I think that John would be all over your mother again if he had a chance. Don't you think you're inviting disaster by seeing so much of him?"

"Grace, I'm beginning to like my father, in spite of his mistakes. I enjoy his company. And you know that my mother can take care of herself. She's not interested in him at all, and he'll catch on to that eventually."

"Okay. Okay. I'll tend to your dog. You just be careful, you hear?" She grabbed Ginny and kissed her quickly on her cheek.

Ginny hoped to be there before darkness set in, but the traffic was heavy most of the way. People were thronging to take in the prime weekend for color. She finally arrived at Calley's Cottage around eight. John met her at the door and gave her a brief hug.

"I'll put your bag in 'your room'," he said, taking her bag.

She followed him down the hall. "So this is to be 'my room', huh? I was pretty nervous when I stayed here before."

"We were both nervous during that visit," he replied, solemnly. "But things are better now, aren't they?"

She smiled. "Much better. Have you eaten? No? So where are we going for dinner? I'm starved."

He led her to the kitchen where wonderful smells competed with a bouquet of aromatic asters on the table, set for two. Steam rose from the skillet, and a huge blueberry cheesecake on the sideboard caught her eye.

"Surprise. I can cook," he said with a big grin. "We're having pepper steak, rice, salad, hot rolls, and, of course, dessert."

She looked amazed. "Did you make all this?"

"Sure. Just kidding. I put the pepper steak on right after you called, but I did run out and pick up the rolls and cheesecake from my favorite bakery."

He sat her down, lit the candles, and served her. She dug in with gusto. The food was delicious, so much so that she was barely able to hold the gorgeous dessert.

"I should have left the cheesecake off," she groaned, as they took their coffee to the porch. He grabbed two sweaters off the hook by the door, and she put one on, pushing up the sleeves that draped over her fingertips. The night air was crisp and smelled of burning leaves.

"This is nice," she said, remembering the other time she sat on this porch with her father, scared and resentful. She relaxed against the wicker swing, glad that things had improved dramatically since then. It felt right to be sitting here with him. He was smiling at her.

"I was on cloud nine after you called. It thrilled me that you wanted to come and spend time with me. Thank you, Ginny."

"It feels right," she said, giving herself a push with her foot. "Whatever happened between you and my mother is past. I've missed having a father. After my grandfather died, there was no male figure around for me, and I missed that. I'm glad that you're in my life now."

He dropped his eyes as emotions filled his chest. "You don't know what that means to me. A few weeks ago, I didn't even know you existed. And now here we are. It's…just wonderful."

They sat in silence for a moment, content to be quiet. Then his face brightened.

"I've been blessed twice over, Ginny. Your mother agreed to have dinner with me last weekend. I drove down, and we had a wonderful time."

Ginny blinked. "What? She hasn't said a word to me when we've talked on the phone."

"Hmmmm. I think I've said too much. She didn't tell me not to tell you though."

"She's probably afraid I'll try to make a big deal of it," Ginny said, grimacing. "Oh, well, I'll act like its news if she does tell me. It's great you two saw each other and had a good time. Maybe you can do it again soon?"

"I hope so. But that's up to your mother. I wouldn't push her on this. I don't have that right."

After an hour of conversation, Ginny's eyes grew heavy, and they called it a night. Snuggled into the downy bed, she fell asleep right away.

The next morning John suggested a ride to a restaurant up on the mountain. They drove about five miles, circling a beautiful lake that shone like a turquoise jewel among the colorful leaves. The small café overlooked the lake, and they dined on a hearty breakfast while watching boats cruising up and down.

Later, they strolled through the streets of Laurel Springs, taking in the shops. At one, she admired an old-fashioned garnet pendant fashioned with tiny garnets that dangled from a larger stone. When she moved on to look at art prints, he bought it for her, and quickly slipped it into his pocket.

Still full from breakfast, they skipped lunch and drove up to the century old hotel and had tea. When they returned to the house, she gingerly asked if it would bother him if he showed her pictures of Calley. He got out the photos, and took her back through the years with his other daughter. He did it without giving in to his usual emotions of sadness, glad to be sharing the memories with Ginny. Ginny was amazed at how much her sibling had looked like her down through the years. It was almost like looking at herself as a child. Though she never knew until recently that Calley existed, she felt a distinct sense of loss.

At the end of the day, they again retired to the porch, content with their long day of getting re-acquainted. They needed no sweaters, even after darkness set in. The night was warm and humid, unusually so.

"We'd better check the weather," he said before they went to their rooms. "This sudden warmth doesn't feel right."

Switching on the TV, they found the weather channel. Rain and a cold front would be moving in Sunday afternoon according to the lithe blonde on the screen. Rain would continue throughout the weekend, ending Monday morning.

Ginny yawned. "I'd better head out early before the rain comes. I don't want to get caught in heavy traffic and rain, too."

"I hate for you to leave, but I want you to be safe," he agreed.

She called Noah after getting ready for bed, and they talked for about an hour, catching up on each other's weekend. He sounded less stressed.

"I have missed you something awful," he said. "What time will you get home?"

"I'm leaving early, so I should be home by eleven. We're supposed to have rain coming in, and I want to miss as much of it as I can," she told him. "I'll be so glad to see you."

"Be sure and leave your phone on, and I'll call you when I get up. I may sleep in before I start home."

She blew a kiss into the phone and turned out her light. It had been a wonderful weekend, but she would be happy to get back home to Noah again. She could hardly wait to see him.

As was her habit, Ginny rose early. Forgoing make-up, she slipped into jeans and tee shirt and put her things together. John had made coffee and insisted she take the time to eat a donut. He sat at the kitchen table across from her.

"This has been a wonderful weekend, Ginny," he said, pouring her another cup of coffee for the road. "I want you to have something to remember it by." He grinned as he brought the pendant out of his pocket and shyly handed it to her.

She opened the box and gasped. "You saw me looking at this, didn't you? You shouldn't have. But it's beautiful. I love it. Thank you so much. Can you fasten it for me?" He fastened it around her neck, and she went to the mirror in the hall. Leaning against the doorframe with folded arms, he watched her turn about to admire the gift.

"Thank you. I'll wear it even with my jeans." She rose on her toes and kissed his cheek, and he smiled, happy to have pleased his lovely daughter.

As he took her bag to the car, the rain began. "You'll get wet," she protested as he opened her door. "Go back in. And thanks for everything. I'll see you soon." He waved as she pulled off; thinking how lonesome the rest of the day would be without her.

She wove through the town, glad that she decided to leave early. The traffic was light as she pulled onto the highway and started the long drive home. Her immediate thoughts were of the connection that had been forged over her visit. She was almost as comfortable with him as she would have been with Grace, and it surprised her. Then she began to imagine her parents on a date. It wasn't really such a stretch; they were both good looking, both young. She lapsed into 'what ifs', smiling at the possibility of them getting together again someday.

About five miles down the road, her daydreams came to an abrupt end. The wind had picked up and was blowing the rain sideways in sheets. She was having difficulty holding the car on the road, and it frightened her. Straining to see, she looked for a side road to pull off on, but she passed two driveways because she couldn't see them in time to turn. Slowing to a crawl, she put the defroster on high to clear the fogged up windows.

As she put her right hand back on the wheel, approaching headlights filled the windshield and the sickening squall of brakes drowned out the pelting rain. She watched the glass shatter as if it was in slow motion, pieces seeming to float in the air, until the crush of the air bag took away her breath, and she felt the car being hurled through the air. The last sound she heard was the horrific crunch of metal as the car flipped down an embankment and smashed against a tree. Then all was silent darkness.

Chapter 20

"Grace? It's Noah."

"Oh, hi, Noah. Are you home?"

"No, I'm still in Louisville. Have you heard from Ginny this morning?"

"No, I haven't. Why? Is something wrong?" Grace clutched the phone with both hands.

"I can't raise her. She was to leave early to avoid the rain, but it's stormy here and even worse where she's coming from according to the TV. She was supposed to have her phone on, and with the bad weather, I can't believe she would leave it off."

"Have you called her father's house?"

"I don't have his number, and it's not listed." He was beginning to sound desperate.

"Okay. Here's Alison's number. She's in Lexington and probably has John's number." Grace read him the number and hung up. She took a deep breath and put her hand to her chest. Assuring herself that Ginny was fine, she tried to fight off the cold feeling in the pit of her stomach. She would wait a few minutes and call Alison herself.

As soon as Noah called Alison, she called the cottage number that John had left.

"John, is Ginny still there, by any chance?"

"She's been gone almost an hour. Why, Alison? What's wrong?"

"Noah has been trying to call but can't reach her. Do you suppose she pulled off somewhere until the rain stopped?"

"There aren't many places to pull off." A loud crack of thunder rattled his nerves. "But I know she had her phone on because I saw her stop to turn it on as she started out to the car."

"Oh, John. I'm getting worried."

"Listen, Alison. There could be a reason why she's not answering. I'm going out and see if I see her car stalled anywhere. I'll call you back in a few minutes. Stay calm."

He grabbed his old worn raincoat from the closet and took the keys from the hook. The rain had let up some, but the lightning was fierce. Long jagged streaks lit up the sky; the very air crackled with electricity. He wished, as he drove through the familiar streets out to the highway, that he had talked her into staying longer. But the rain wasn't supposed to hit until afternoon. He looked from side to side, thinking she might have stopped for gas or just to wait out the storm.

Turning onto the highway, he drove slowly, looking down every crossroad he came to. The rain came in waves, slacking up, then pouring again. After driving for several miles, he was ready to give up and turn back when the traffic slowed and finally came to a stop. Through the misty blur of the rain, he could see the whirling lights reflected in the tops of the cars. Frantically, he pulled off the road as far as he could and took off running. As he passed the cars in front of his, he could see two state police cars and an ambulance just around the curve. It hit him, as he ran, the old familiar pain in his chest. This was only a short distance from the spot where his family was killed.

"Please don't let this be Ginny," he prayed as he reached the policeman who was trying to direct traffic around a pick-up truck with the front bashed in. He grabbed the policeman's arm.

"What happened here?" He yelled over the noise of the rain and the commotion.

The patrolman frowned and pulled his arm away. "Go back to your car, sir. We're trying to get an emergency team in here. A woman is trapped in the vehicle down in the ravine."

John looked down the embankment, and began to scream. "NO–NO–NOOOO." He slid down the slope, losing his footing and falling part of the way, sliding in the mud and wet leaves. Another patrolman at Ginny's car yelled, "Go back. Help is on the way."

"She's my daughter," he shouted as he reached the mangled mess of her car. He could barely see her slumped over in the seat, the air bag limply hanging over her.

There was blood on her face, and the sole of her foot was at a crazy angle. She wasn't moving.

"Ginny, Ginny!" He screamed as he pulled on the door, but it was crushed and wouldn't open. The patrolman tried to pull him back, but John kept trying to open the door.

"Sir, we can't get the car door open to get her out. There's an emergency team on the way with equipment that will open the door. Please try and calm yourself... Oh, my God. I remember you. Your wife and daughter...I was at that accident, too. I'll never forget that one. Man, I'm so sorry. Here, take this handkerchief. You cut your hand." John waved it away and wiped his hands on his wet jeans. They both looked up as the equipment truck labored its way to the edge of the drop off.

The patrolman took John by the arm and helped him up the bank. "Are you okay, sir? Here, sit in the car out of the way while they do their work. You can't help her until we get her out."

John obediently climbed in and rolled down the window to watch. His hands were trembling, his mind flashing from the horrible accident of the past to the present one. He began to pray, chanting over and over, "Please let her live. Please let her live."

The truck maneuvered down the bank, getting as close to Ginny's car as they could. It seemed forever to John, but they had the huge jaws in place quickly. They closed on the car and began to rip it open. John held his breath until he saw them reach in and slide a brace under Ginny, carefully securing it and slowly bring her out of the wreckage. He jumped from the patrol car and started down the slope as they were bringing her up to the ambulance.

"I'm her father. I'm going with her," he said to the EMT.

"Give me your keys, I'll get your car to the hospital," the patrolman said, and John pitched them to him as they closed the ambulance doors.

The technicians gently moved him aside to a side seat as they began to work over Ginny. He watched their every move, softly saying her name over and over. The sound of the siren as they flew down the wet road brought him to his senses. He hadn't called Alison back. He punched in her number with trembling fingers.

Chapter 21

The surgical waiting room of the small hospital was empty; all non-essential surgeries were scheduled for weekdays. The storm had knocked out power and generators were providing light for the doctor and nurses who were working to set Ginny's broken ankle. Other tests would have to wait until full power was restored.

John sat wearily in the green leather chair. He had paced the floor until his bad leg began to throb. There were no volunteers at this time on Sunday, but a nurse's aide had made a pot of coffee and tried to get him to get something to eat from the goodie basket provided by one of the churches. He agreed to the coffee and now sat nursing the mug when Alison and Noah burst into the room.

"Where is she?" Alison shouted, grabbing his arm, causing coffee to splatter on the gray tile floor.

Noah took her by the shoulders. "Sit down here, that's right. Now let's give John a chance to tell us."

"I'm sorry," she murmured, clumsily wiping at the coffee on John's shirt. "Tell us how she is."

"I don't know; I wish I did. Right now, they are setting her broken ankle. The doctor says she's in shock, drifting in and out of consciousness. They have to do a CAT scan because there is some internal bleeding, but the storm has knocked out power so they'll have to wait for that. We can see her when they're finished with the ankle."

Alison was pale; tear tracks made lines down her face and her smeared eye-make-up made dark circles. She clasped her hands and tried to listen calmly as John told them about coming upon the wreck and the ride to the hospital. Noah sat with his head in his hands.

"This is a small hospital. Will they be able to care for her properly here? Should we have her moved to a larger hospital where they have more…"

"It is small, but remember they care for a lot of people when the population swells in the summer. There are good doctors here. But, of course, if necessary we can move her. Let's pray she isn't hurt that badly." John was wrestling to keep down his own anxiety.

Alison got up and began to pace. "How could you let her leave in this storm?" she demanded of John. "What possessed you to allow her to start home? Are you crazy?"

"It wasn't storming when she first left, Alison. We didn't expect heavy rain until later on in the day. Of course, I wouldn't have let her start home if I had known it would hit so fast and so hard."

She shook her head and sat down beside him. He took her hand, and she locked her fingers tightly with his. Three pairs of eyes watched the door hopefully, as time seemed to drag. Finally, a tall, lanky, green-coated young doctor looked around the door.

"Cantrell family?" They jumped to attention, and he motioned them back down as he dragged a chair to face them. "You're her parents? And brother?"

"Fiancé," Noah corrected without giving the word a second thought.

"I'm Dr. Logan. Ginny has several injuries: broken ribs, broken foot and ankle. We've set the ankle and sewed up some cuts on her face and arms. That's the good news. There is some internal bleeding, and we need to find out what's going on there. Since we're back on full power, we're going to go ahead with the tests now."

"Is she going to be okay? I mean…she's going to live, isn't she?" Alison sobbed through the question.

"We'll do all we can to make sure she lives. And we'll have more to tell you later. Now would you like to see her, just for a moment? We're going to take her down for scans, and you can see her as they pass. Come with me." He led them into the hall where nurses were pushing a gurney toward the service elevator.

Alison rushed to the side and looked down at her daughter, gasping when she saw the battered face. The left side was grotesquely swollen, slick and red like a burn, and the eye already blue and closed.

"That's mostly air bag injuries," Dr. Logan patted Alison's shoulder. "Time will take care of that."

"Has she been conscious?" John asked.

"She woke up when we were setting the ankle, but she went out again. She's still in shock. Now we'd better get her down for the tests." He waved the nurses on. "You can wait up here or in the big waiting room downstairs. It's more comfortable there."

Noah caught the gurney before they rolled it onto the elevator and kissed the top of Ginny's head. He heard a soft moan escape her lips, and the pitiful sound clutched at his heart. His eyes watched as the doors closed, half believing that she called his name. As they all turned back to the waiting room, the elevator opened again, and a nurse thrust a package in his hands.

"Here are the things she had on. You might want to keep them; there's some jewelry in there."

He handed the bundle to Alison. After an emotional moment, she released the drawstring and looked inside. She sobbed when she saw the blood-stained blouse and touched the stains. Sticking out of the folds was a plastic bag with Ginny's jewelry, the simple gold loop earrings, her watch, and the garnet pendant.

The time seemed to drag as they waited for more news. The gloom outside lifted and welcome sunlight left a shadow across the floor. John rose and went to the window, touching the pane. It was cold with the chill the rain had bought. Water still ran into the storm drains and stood in puddles on the parking lot. Leaves covered the grass, leaving bare limbs black against the sky. He sighed. If only Ginny had waited to leave.

"Good news!" Dr. Logan bounced into the room. "Things look better than we first thought. The internal bleeding has abated now. We'll do a kidney x-ray when she's s little stronger, maybe Tuesday. She's alert and in some pain, but we can start her on medication for that now that we know there's no serious head injury. She's back in a room, so you may go in. Just don't tire her out. Questions?"

"We haven't even asked about the other driver. How is…"

"He walked away with only scratches, which is miraculous because he's a seventy year old man."

After many questions, they were assured that Ginny was in good hands. Anxiously, they went right to her room. She was tethered to IVs and tubes; her leg incased in an air cast on top of the sheet. Her face looked even worse in the bright light over her bed.

"Hi, honey," Alison whispered, reaching under the sheet for her hand and squeezed. Ginny squeezed back. She tried to talk, but her lips were too swollen and painful to move. She reached out with one hand to John and then to Noah, and they took turns telling her that she would be fine and that they loved her. Sighing she closed her eyes and drifted off just as the nurse came in to apply ointment to her face.

"I didn't realize that air bags could do so much damage," Alison said to the nurse as she worked.

"But it probably saved her life," the nurse replied. "You're her mother? You'll want to stay with her, I'm sure. She needs to drink liquids as often as she can, and she'll need help with the straw since she can't open her mouth very wide." She smiled at the two men. "I know she'll be happy to see you guys tomorrow, but right now she needs her mom more."

Alison pulled the chair up to the bed, rested her chin on the bed rail, unable to take her eyes from Ginny's face. John and Noah slipped out quietly and left them alone.

Chapter 22

Alison sat straight up in bed and fumbled for the light. It took a few seconds for her to realize where she was even as the lamp shed its light on the lovely bedroom. She was in Calley's Cottage in the same room where Ginny stayed, so John had told her. Sinking back into the pillows, she glanced at the clock—five o'clock. She had slept all night for the first time since Ginny's accident.

After they had gotten the word from Dr. Logan late Wednesday that Ginny's kidneys were functioning normally, John had taken Alison back to his house to get some much needed rest. It was the only time she had left the hospital, and she didn't let herself feel strange about staying at John's house. She was too grateful for a soft bed instead of the clumsy foldout chair.

Ginny was feeling much better. Her soreness and pain had eased, though her broken ribs kept her from being comfortable in bed. Soon they would have her up on crutches. The skinned portion of her face had scabbed over in places, and the swelling had diminished, her eye open again. She had insisted that her mother go get some rest. Since Noah had to go back to work, Ginny wanted some time alone with him before he would drive back in the wee hours of the morning.

Turning the lamp off, Alison laid in the semi-darkness saying a prayer of thanks for Ginny's progress. Then she closed her eyes and tried to doze, but sleep would not return. So she got up and showered, relishing the hot steam and fragrant guest soap John had provided. Slipping into the terry robe hanging on the door, she went to get her clothes out of the dryer, thankful that she had taken time last night to wash them. The aroma of brewing coffee lured her into the kitchen.

She found John slicing melon. "Good morning. I thought you were going to stay with Ginny until I got there this morning."

"She ran me off," he said, with a grin. "Said she needed a little time to herself. Noah stayed until about one o'clock, and I sat with her until three. She rolled over and said, 'John, go home.'"

"Miss Independent," Alison said, eyeing the coffeepot. "Is that ready yet?"

He poured two cups and put the melon and a coffeecake on the table. Alison shook her head when he offered her the food but ended up eating three slices of melon and a big slice of the cake.

"Guess I was hungrier than I thought. Thanks for providing the robe and the laundry and the wonderful bed. I slept like a log."

"You needed it, you were exhausted. And you can keep the robe, its part of the service." he smiled.

"John, do you ever think about starting your bed and breakfast back up again?"

"Lately I have. For a long time I thought I would never get back in the business. It's a two-person operation, usually a couple, although others have managed with hired help. Would you like to see the house? You hardly saw it last night when I brought you home... um...here."

"I've always loved this kind of house," she remarked as he took her through the rambling cottage. "Sometimes I get unhappy with my small apartment and think about buying something. Then I think about upkeep, and the urge goes away."

She paused. "Well, I must get back to the hospital whether Ginny wants peace and quiet or not. I have to be there."

"I'll take you whenever you're ready."

When they arrived at the hospital, they found Dr. Logan in Ginny's room.

"Our patient is doing extremely well," he said with a smile. "It's up on crutches today, and if she manages okay on them, she can go home."

"Home? Already? She lives four hours away, Doctor. Of course, I could take her home with me. That's only an hour or so away."

"I forgot that you don't all live here," Dr. Logan said with a frown.

"She can stay at the cottage. I live close by. Then she won't have to make the trip to her place until she's stronger," John exclaimed. "That's okay, isn't it, Alison? And you can stay, too, can't you? I mean...your job..."

Alison bit her lip. She hadn't expected Ginny to leave until she was completely ready to travel. As she hesitated, Ginny made the decision.

"John's house sounds great to me. I'd love to be in a regular bed. And you don't have to go back to work yet, do you, Mom?"

"No. I've got time coming to me. Sure, if that's okay with John. But four days in the hospital, as badly as you were hurt..."

"She can recuperate there as well as she can here. We'll get these tubes out right now. And if she does okay on her crutches, and you can take her to your house tonight," Dr. Logan told John.

"How long will it be before she's ready to travel back to her own place, Doctor?" Alison asked.

"Well, that depends on how she gets along. I want to see her in a week, and we'll go from there. First, the crutches. I'll send the therapist in with a pair. Ginny, with the sore ribs, it will be uncomfortable at first."

Ginny grinned. "I can do it, Doc. You just watch."

But it was difficult. She only got halfway down the hall before she was exhausted and had to be helped back to bed.

"It takes a while," the therapist said as she pulled up the sheet. "Just take it a little at a time. When your ribs mend, it won't be so painful. And you're still weak, young lady."

Ginny felt like crying. She was so ready to leave the hospital. Later, when they saw Dr. Logan again, he suggested that he might have rushed her, and that they should give it another day. Ginny kept on working through the pain the next day, and Friday morning, they loaded her up and drove to Calley's Cottage.

John was excited. He had a lady to come in and clean, and the house smelled fresh. He made a big pot of soup and brought fresh bread and a cake from the bakery. Fresh linens were on the bed in Ginny's room, and he moved in a recliner. There were even fresh flowers in the living room and by the patient's bed.

"Everything looks so nice," Ginny exclaimed as they settled her in the recliner. "You've gone to so much trouble."

"It was no trouble. I'm so happy to have you both here." John beamed at them. "You're in this room, Alison." He took her down the hall to a bedroom with antique furniture and rose patterned wallpaper. There were white roses in a vase by the bed. Alison sighed. Her misgivings disappeared, and she smiled at him. "Thank you, John. Being here is really a blessing. Now would you mind if I took your car and went shopping? Neither Ginny nor I have anything else to wear."

She drove to the shopping center where John directed her and bought gowns and a loose dress for Ginny and things for herself. When she got back, John had lunch ready. Ginny insisted on eating at the table, and though it took some maneuvering, they made her comfortable. She ate like a starving man.

"So good," Ginny sighed as she took the last bite of lemon cake. "Hospital food was okay, but this is wonderful. If you keep feeding me like this, I'll be well in no time—and fat, too." But she soon tired and they helped her back to bed.

"And you," he said to Alison, "are to get a nap yourself. I'm on call in case Ginny needs anything." He shooed her from the room.

As Alison lay down on the feather bed and drew an afghan over her, she thought how nice it was to have an attentive man to spoil her. It was something a woman could get used to.

Chapter 23

During the next few days, Ginny began to grow more and more lethargic. Her chipper mood on being released from the hospital gave way to moodiness and silence. Alison and John didn't know quite what to make of it. When they asked her what was wrong, she couldn't tell them. So they called Dr. Logan. He was concerned, but not surprised.

"Sometimes after a trauma, depression sets in, even when a patient is doing well physically. Give her a few days. If she isn't better, I may prescribe medication. We'll hold off on seeing her again until the middle of the week. I'd like to see this clear up naturally."

When Alison hung up, she was frowning. She told John what the doctor had said. Since he had dealt with depression himself after his family's accident, he understood much better than Alison.

Noah came for the weekend, but still Ginny remained in her own little shell. It shook Noah up when she didn't respond to his loving words but only nodded and listened politely and seemed worlds away.

He had the antique ring that had belonged to his mother and grandmother in his pocket. His plan was to propose to Ginny, hoping she would say 'yes', and they could share the excitement together, the joy that could possibly help her heal faster. Now he pulled it out and slid it on his little finger as he discussed Ginny with her parents.

"It's a beautiful ring, Noah," Alison said as she watched him twirl it on his finger. "But hold on to it for awhile. The doctor says this isn't too unusual. Let's give her a little time."

Noah was badly disappointed. He had imagined her response a thousand times. She would throw her arms around him and tell him how badly she wanted to be his wife. But Ginny was so listless and oblivious to his attentiveness that the ring never left his pocket.

"There was no head injury, was there?" he asked John. "I mean she doesn't seem like herself at all. This is just so sudden. I don't understand."

John handed Noah a jacket, and said, "Let's walk."

As they strolled in the chilly evening air, John told Noah a little about his own bout with depression. "I know how Ginny feels. It could be that she is just now reliving the accident. I know I'm still reliving it myself, seeing her smashed against that tree. It hits me every time I lie down to sleep. She may snap out of it in a few days, but, if she doesn't, we'll take her back to Dr. Logan for medication. She'll be okay, Noah, she really will."

"Poor, sweet Ginny. I'll try to be more patient. I just knew that my proposing to her would make her so happy. But she's not ready for that, and it can wait until she's better. I love her so much." John put his hand on Noah's shoulder to comfort him as they turned back toward the house, red and gold leaves crunching under their feet.

The weekend passed with Ginny staying mostly in bed. Alison coaxed her into walking on the crutches every day, but she gave it minimal effort. Noah was almost as depressed when he had to leave on Sunday. All the way home, he let his imagination run away with him. What if she didn't love him anymore? What if the accident changed her so much that she didn't want to be a part of his life? He spent a sleepless night, and when the alarm went off bright and early on Monday morning, he felt like he had been in the accident with her.

Back in Laurel Springs, Ginny had made no improvement by the time of her appointment. Dr. Logan checked her over and found her healing, her cuts and bruises fading. He let her dress, then seated her in his office.

"You don't seem like you did when you left the hospital, Ginny. Are you having pain somewhere that you haven't told me about?"

"No, nothing different. I wake up at night and can't go back to sleep, and when that happens, I ache and can't get comfortable."

"Do you sleep during the day?"

"No. Sometimes I doze, but I don't really sleep."

"You're not walking much, are you? Ginny, you won't get your strength back if you don't exert yourself a little bit." He patted her hand to take the sting out of his remark.

"I know, but I just can't seem to make myself get up and do it. I don't know why. It's like I'm just tied to the bed."

After more questions, Dr. Logan prescribed a mild antidepressant, and John and Alison took her home.

For a few days, there didn't seem to be any change. They rented funny movies, took her on rides, made jokes out of every little thing that came up. Alison began to despair. She had a job that she had to get back to soon, yet she couldn't leave her daughter.

"I don't know what to do," she told John as they sat on the porch while darkness crept into the mountains. Ginny was already in bed, and it was only eight thirty.

"If you need to get back to work, leave her here. I'll work with the doctor. I feel like he'll get this straightened out soon. If this medication doesn't work, he'll try something else."

She sighed. "You know I can't leave, John. Not without her. I know you would take the very best care of her, but I'm her mother." Tears welled up in her eyes. He stood and moved over beside her on the swing and gently pulled her over against his shoulder. He felt her stiffen, then relax. She rested there until he leaned and gently brought his lips down on hers. The response was electric; she returned his kiss with fervor, turning and twisting her arms around his neck. Then suddenly she pulled away.

"John, no. We can't do this."

"I'm sorry. I meant to comfort you. No, that's not true. I've wanted to do that since I saw you at Ginny's. And even before…"

"Stop! It's just been so long since I've been kissed, that's all. I'm sorry, too. But we have to think of Ginny now."

"Why? Why can't we think of ourselves, too? Because of me, we wasted a lot of years when we could have been together."

"You had a good marriage, John. I was a single mother."

"Yes, it was a good marriage, but it's over. You had Ginny alone, and she's an adult now. With all my heart I'd like to start over again. I know I have no right to ask you to let go of the past. But we've changed, we're different people."

"I'll have to leave if you keep saying things like that, John. It puts a strain on what has become a very pleasant relationship." She rose to go inside.

"But you kissed me back, Alison. I thought for a moment you still had feelings for me." He said to her stiff back as he followed her back into the house. She went to Ginny's door and opened it slightly. Ginny was sleeping with the light on, a book face down beside her. Closing the door, Alison turned to face John.

"You've been wonderful to us. I don't know what I would have done with out you. But now I think it would be best if I took Ginny home, back to her house. I can stay with her for a few days before I go back to work.

Maybe being there with her dog will help. She's missed Grover terribly."

John sighed. Disappointment was evident in his reply. "You may be right, it might help. I hope you're not doing this because ..."

"No, honestly. I was going to mention this to you. We'll talk to the doctor tomorrow, and if he agrees, I'll take her home. You may come whenever you wish. You know, she's come to think so highly of you."

He wanted to snap at her for being so condescending. Being Ginny's father had come so rapidly into his life, and in a short time, he had almost lost her. Now he couldn't imagine his life without her.

Chapter 24

Having received the go-ahead from Dr. Logan, John helped Alison load the rental car the next morning. They made Ginny comfortable in the back seat with pillows to raise her cast and cushion her back.

"It's a beautiful morning to drive," he said, trying to inject a note of cheer into his voice. Inwardly, he was aching as he helped them prepare to leave. He leaned in and gave Ginny an awkward hug. "Goodbye, honey. Take care of yourself. I'll be down to see you in a few days."

She patted his cheek. "Thank you so much for everything. You've taken such good care of us." Tears began to trickle down her cheeks.

"Hey, none of that. You're worth everything to me. I'll see you soon. Chin up, hear?" He backed off before his face gave him away.

"John, what can I say?" Alison gave him a quick hug, and he didn't try to hold her. She smiled as she buckled her seat belt and waved as they slowly pulled away.

He watched them until they were around the corner, then turned to go back into his empty house. How lonesome it would be without them. He wished they could have stayed until Ginny was better. In a few days, he would drive down and check on her. He closed the door with a sigh, dreading the silent hours ahead.

The ride home was uneventful. Ginny didn't seem to be nervous about being in a car again. When they came close to the place where the accident occurred, she raised up to see if she would remember the spot. Alison knew when she saw the black marks on the highway and the still visible ruts down the bank that this was probably the location, but she said nothing to Ginny, and they passed it without slowing down.

After the long quiet drive, they finally pulled into the driveway. Alison had called Grace before leaving, and she and Grover were on the porch to welcome them home.

"Here's my girl," Grace exclaimed as she opened the car door. Grover's barking was deafening. The two got Ginny up on her crutches and helped her slowly up the steps. Grover bounded ahead, his tail going around in circles.

Ginny went slowly from room to room as if she hadn't seen them in a long, long time. Grace guided her to the back bedroom. "I've fixed this room for you, honey, so you won't have to climb those stairs for awhile." Grace opened the door to the room with freshly painted peach colored walls. There were vases of flowers on every table.

Ginny gasped. "Where on earth…"

"Noah fixed up this room," Grace said with a smile. "He said you liked daises, so he had them put in every arrangement."

"How sweet." Ginny gazed around the room in awe. But the drive had taken its toll, and she allowed them to fuss over her and settle her into the bed for a quick nap. Grace and Alison left her, calling Grover to follow. But she called, "let Grover stay with me." She patted the bed, and Grover settled down next to her carefully avoiding the cast as if he knew he might hurt her.

In the kitchen, Grace poured hot tea for Alison. "Tell me everything. How is she? Her face seems to be better although it's still rather slick looking."

"Yeah, but I don't think it will require surgery. She's healing fine, Grace, but she's still so depressed. Would you spend as much time with her as you can? You're so good with her."

Grace smiled. "Sure, I'll be over here as much as she wants. Maybe she's been coddled long enough by you and John and needs a firmer hand. She's never been one for self pity before."

"No, but she's never had a trauma like this before. You'll know what to say and do, though. Dr. Logan says she'll come out of this soon, and I hope he's right. I need to go back to work, but I'm going to call and ask for a little more time. I may lose my job, but that's okay. I can find another one."

Ginny was just getting up and moving around when Noah came over that evening. He took her in his arms, and she let go of the crutches and held on to him.

"The flowers are so beautiful," she said as he carried her awkwardly to the sofa. "I lay there all afternoon just inhaling their fragrance."

He turned her face to his and kissed her. "Nothing is too good for my girl. I've missed you so much, honey."

She smiled. "Me, too." But the old light in her eyes wasn't there.

Grace had prepared a big homecoming meal, but Ginny was only able to eat a small portion. Then she asked Noah to excuse her because she was tired, and he kissed her good night as Grace and Alison stood to help her to her room.

"No," she said firmly. "I can make it on my own. I'll see you in the morning." She moved slowly to avoid Grover's exuberant wiggling at her side and they disappeared into the bedroom.

"Sorry, Noah." Alison sat beside him on the sofa. "It's going to take more time, I guess."

"I've got time," he assured her.

As the days passed, they started to see subtle changes in Ginny. She began to exercise more, with Grace's insistence, and to watch TV instead of just lying in bed. Grace insisted that she work at least one crossword puzzle a day and brought Ginny an armful of books from the library. Her perfunctory smile was becoming genuine.

Dr. Madison was seeing her often and keeping a check on her medicine. "She's coming along," he told

Alison. "I'm going to reduce the dosage just a little and see how she does. I think she'll be less sleepy."

By the time Ginny was ready to get rid of her big cast, she was almost the old Ginny, much to everyone's relief. She was now in a walking cast and seldom needed her crutches.

John, who had made a trip down ten days before, had been invited by both Ginny and Alison for Thanksgiving. He had seen some improvement the previous trip, but this time, the change was dramatic. Both Ginny and her mother were more relaxed.

"You've worked wonders with Ginny," he said to Grace.

"Huh! I just make her toe the line, unlike you and her mother," Grace snapped. But she smiled as she turned her head away.

She and Alison had made a feast, with some help from Ginny. Noah came in with a big beautiful arrangement for the table, and Ginny greeted him with a big hug.

"Sweetheart, your florist bill is going to be outrageous. These are so lovely." She fingered the colored leaves, goldenrod, asters, and dried seed pods artfully arranged in a ceramic pumpkin.

"Actually, a co-worker arranged this for me. This is Mom's pumpkin that she used for years on our table."

Ginny grabbed him and held him close. "In all this ado about my wreck, we forgot that you are still grieving for your mother. I'm sorry, darling."

He tightened his arms around her and kissed her until he had to pull away to catch his breath.

"You don't know how glad I am to see you so cheerful again. I was so worried about you," he whispered.

"I'll keep on taking my medicine; it's helped me so much. I've had too much spoiling from everyone. It's time I got well and did for others, including you, you've had no attention from me."

He grinned. "I'm fine now that you are."

Grace opened the French doors leading into the dining room. "It's on the table. Everybody come on." She eyed John with her usual caution, then reluctantly smiled at him. "John, you come take the chair at the head of the table."

"Thank you, Grace. If you don't mind, I'd like to ask the blessing. We all have so many things to be thankful for this year." They gathered around the table and joined hands. John began a prayer of thanks for his daughter, for her health, for the healing relationship with Alison, for Noah, and for Grace—a prayer so elegant that even Grace had tears in her eyes.

As they sat down to their meal, an early snow began to cover the remainder of the fallen leaves and turned the dreary landscape into a fairy land of white crystals. Even though it was too warm for it to stick very long, the big flakes quickly covered the ground, making the world seem bright and new.

Chapter 25

The chilly, musty air struck Alison in the face as she stepped into the small apartment, set down her bag, and turned on the light. Immediately, she heard a gruff "meow", and Monroe ran from the kitchen, tail aloft. She picked him up and buried her face in his soft gray fur.

"Oh, Monroe, sweet kitty. I'm so glad to see you. Did you miss me?" He wiggled to be put down and turned away. "You're mad at me for leaving you, aren't you? Did Mrs. Keane take good care of you while I was gone?" She sniffed. From the smell, she knew the litter box hadn't been changed very often.

It was still warm when she left to go to Ginny, and the furnace was turned off. She shivered in her coat as she reprogrammed the thermostat. Picking up her bag, she went into her bedroom and began to hang up her clothes and put away her cosmetics. Monroe repented and came back, winding around her legs and making welcome sounds in his raspy voice.

Once things were put away, the heat came on and the rooms began to warm up. She removed her coat and went to the kitchen to make a cup of tea. While the microwave hummed, she took the offensive litter box to the trash can and scrubbed it quickly with soap and water, filling it with fresh litter. Monroe meowed approvingly. There was plenty of cat food in his dish so she knew her neighbor had not let him go hungry. She fumbled under the sink for a can of air freshener and went over the apartment spraying vanilla scented mist. Satisfied that the smell was covered up somewhat, she lit a fragrant candle to finish the job. Taking her tea to the sofa, she curled up with Monroe on her lap. Her thoughts drifted back to the time she had been away. It had been only a few weeks, but it seemed like forever as she watched her daughter recover.

Ginny had gone back to work that morning even before the short cast had come off. Alison had wanted her to wait a little longer, but Ginny was anxious to get back to her students. It was so good to see the old Ginny again. Unless she was out with Noah, she would probably be home. Picking up the phone, Alison punched in the number. Ginny answered on the second ring.

"Hi. Just wanted to let you know I'm home. How did it go today at school?"

"Oh, Mom, it went great. They had a welcome back cake, and everybody seemed to be so glad to see me, especially the kids. I got more hugs around the legs today than I've ever gotten before." She laughed, and it was the old Ginny laugh again.

"Aren't you awfully tired?"

"Yeah, I am, but it was just so good to be back. I'll get stronger every day." She paused, then added softly, "Mom, I wouldn't have made it without you and John. I'll never forget all that you've done for me."

Alison smiled. "Sweetheart, as long as I'm breathing, I'll be there for you. You don't need to thank me. And I'm sure John feels the same."

"I know. I'm truly blessed. Oh, Noah just came in. We're going out for an early supper. Then I'm going to crawl in bed with a good book so I'll be rested for tomorrow."

"Okay, I'll let you go. Say hello to Noah for me."

After hanging up, she felt loneliness creep over her. She had been with Ginny, Noah, and Grace for so long. Now they seemed a million miles away from her. She missed Ginny's house, the house they both grew up in. John's cottage had been so comfortable and cozy. Her little pad seemed cold and lifeless.

She thought of John and how kind he had been. Even after they left his house and his wonderful care, he had driven down twice a week to help cheer Ginny. She must call him after she fixed herself a little something to eat.

Opening the refrigerator, she faced containers of gray hairy remnants of long ago meals. Turning up her nose at the thought of dealing with the mess, she decided to heat up a can of soup to give her a little energy and browse through the mail Mrs. Keane had left on the hall table. As the soup warmed, she looked out the window at the darkness. Usually she didn't mind the early winter nightfall; it was cozy to eat early and cuddle under a quilt with a good book. Tonight it seemed oppressive and heavy around her.

After washing up her dinner dishes, she forced herself to clean the refrigerator, tossing out food with lightning speed. As she gave the counters and sinks a final wipe, the phone rang.

"Hi, Alison."

"Hello, John. I was going to give you a ring later. How are you?"

"Fine. Just wanted to check on you. I talked to Ginny. She had just gotten home from having dinner with Noah. She seems to be her old self, all bubbly over her first day back at school."

"Yeah, she was happy to see her kids. She's a great teacher, you know."

"You sound just a little bit down. Anything wrong?"

Alison winced. She hadn't meant for her voice to betray her. "Well, I guess I am a little down. This apartment seemed so empty when I walked in. If Monroe hadn't been here to greet me, I think I would have turned around and gone back to Ginny's."

"I know what you mean. That's how I felt when you both left Laurel Springs. It's hard to go from being a caretaker to being alone again."

"Right. Well, I'll get back in the swing of things tomorrow when I have to go back to work." She almost felt revulsion at the thought.

"Look, why don't I drive over Saturday? We'll go to the State Park and have dinner, maybe do a little

Christmas shopping first. You can help me find something to give Ginny for Christmas."

She grew quiet, wondering if this was a good idea. Would it give him false hopes? If she said no, she would be alone all weekend. And alone was something she didn't want to be right now.

"Okay. That sounds like a plan. What time can I expect you?"

Chapter 26

On a cold, crisp Saturday, Alison and John set out on their Christmas shopping expedition. In stores aglitter and swathed in greenery, carols played repetitiously in the background. The cheer in the air was contagious, and they wandered with the maze of shoppers, laughing and talking. After looking their way through a few stores, the pair stopped for a cup of coffee and sat on a bench watching the children line up for pictures with Santa. A little blue-eyed blond child clung to her mother's skirts. The closer they moved up the line, the more she hid her little face behind the dress.

"I took Ginny to see Santa when she was two," she told John.

"Did she give him a list a mile long?"

"No. She screamed and screamed. She was terrified. It took a lot of talking to get her back for a picture. I'll show it to you sometime. She looks like she's in awful pain, but she's trying to smile."

"Have you seen anything she might like for Christmas?"

"Those sweaters we looked at were lovely. She watches her budget and doesn't buy much for herself. She could use clothes. But I have a better idea."

"Tell me." John pulled her arm through his.

"She adores that antique pendant you gave her. Maybe we could find some earrings to go with it."

"I thought about that, even went back where I bought the pendant, but they didn't have any garnet earrings. And I couldn't remember if it was silver or gold."

"It's silver, and I think I can help you match it. I looked it over pretty good with the idea of buying earrings myself."

"Oh, if you want to get them…"

"No, no. I can get her clothes. I know what she likes. There's a place downtown that sells estate jewelry. That might be a place to look."

They drove from the mall to a small store beside a bakery where the air was heavy with the smell of cinnamon and fresh bread.

"Buy you a loaf of bread, Madam?" With a knightly flourish, he opened the door, and they delighted in the sights and smells of the cakes and pies, cookies and breads. In the end, they settled for two loaves of wheat bread. Alison looked longingly at the brownies, but forced herself to turn away.

"With Christmas coming, I'm bound to gain ten pounds from all the baked stuff."

He smiled at her. "On you, it would look good."

Entering the small jewelry shop that was devoid of Christmas décor but bright with counters of vintage jewels, bags, and collectibles, they looked through old jewelry. They found garnet earrings, but they didn't come close to a match for Ginny's pendant. As they were about to leave, the owner, Mr. Prince, looking antique himself, came from the back of the store with a box.

"Wait. I have something that might interest you. Here's a box of pieces that we just got yesterday. I haven't priced them yet. There are amethysts and garnets and other stones in here." He set the box on the counter, and Alison and John gently sifted through the beautiful old pieces. They reached for the earrings at the same time.

"Perfect. I think these will be a close match," Alison said as she held them up to her ears for John to see. Her dark eyes sparkled, and he had difficulty taking his own eyes from her lovely face.

"I'll take them," he said, nodding as Mr. Prince quoted a price. They were carefully polished by the little man and quickly wrapped in beautiful gold foil paper.

When they stepped back into the crisp air, John said, "Mission accomplished! So what would you like to look for next?"

"To tell the truth, smelling these wonderful smells from the bakery made me hungry. Let's drive up to the park."

They left the small town and drove the crooked roads to the park. An old lodge, built in the twenties of local stone, sat high on a hill. Smoke wafted up from the huge chimneys, the lake gleamed behind it like a jewel in the setting sunlight. A huge Christmas tree stood at attention just inside the door, decorated with frosted apples and red-checked ribbons. The delicious aroma of frying fish and onions drew them into the dining room.

Since it was still early, the cavernous room was almost empty, so they chose a place by the window where they could look out on the water and see the pinks and oranges of the sunset. The buffet was enormous and they feasted on fried catfish, hushpuppies and the trimmings, ending with homemade carrot cake. John ate manly servings of everything. "This is my ten pounds," he said as he went back for seconds.

As they drank their coffee and watched the twilight settle on the fog rising from the lake, John reached across the table for her hand.

"This has been a fun day," he said. "I've missed you…and Ginny, too. I got so used to you when you both were at the cottage. But I'm so thankful she's on the mend."

"It was sweet of you to come so often and check on her, John." She didn't try to remove her hand, but let it lay comfortably in his. She found herself avoiding his eyes and instead concentrated on their hands.

"Having lost a daughter, I can't tell you how much I appreciate having Ginny in my life. I would do anything for her…and for you, too, Alison. I know you don't want to hear this, but I must say it." He took a deep breath. She was smiling at him, waiting, when an enormous crash came from the kitchen. A cacophony of voices scolded the unfortunate person responsible for the noise.

"Someone dropped something big," she said, laughing. "Now what was it that I wouldn't want to hear?"

He stumbled over his words. "You and I–I need to tell you that…"

"It has been a lovely day, John. Anything more than that we shouldn't even be considering." She laughed nervously. "That sounds a bit silly when I'm not sure what you were going to say, but–well- you know what I mean. NO serious talk."

He slowly withdrew his hand and checked his watch to cover up his disappointment. He had so wanted to tell her how much he loved her and beg her to start over with him, to try again. But he could feel her distancing herself, feel her fear of hearing about love and trust, the trust that he had once broken. It seemed to him that there was no way to fix it.

"Why don't we take a walk down to the lake before it gets too dark?"

She rose, and he helped her on with her coat at the door. She knew by his face that she had hurt his feelings and felt a knot in her chest that swelled like a balloon. She wanted to cry. The day had been perfect, and she had ruined it for him. But she couldn't take them back; the words she spoke out of fear of becoming too intimate. She wanted to tell him that she loved him still, that she never really stopped. But it wouldn't work between them. There was no way it would work with their history.

They walked to the sandy shore in silence until a chilly wind picked up, and they pulled up their collars and went briskly to the car. The ride home was filled with aimless chatter about the past election, Ginny, Alison's job–anything to fill up the moments until he left her at her door with a quick kiss on the cheek.

"Christmas? At Ginny's?" she called to him as the elevator opened.

"Sure. See you then." He waved.

She closed her door and leaned against it, unaware that she had crushed the loaf of bread in her arms.

Chapter 27

Noah took a critical look around his living room. Everything was in place. The tree glittered with white lights, the fire burned brightly in the fireplace, candles were ready to light, and the champagne was chilling. Take out Chinese was keeping warm in the oven. He gave a sigh of satisfaction and checked his pocket; the ring was still there.

He had been gone for two days, but even so, he had most of the decorations complete. Grace was keeping Ginny occupied until he had everything ready. She knew he was having dinner for her but expected a casual pizza dinner that he would order before he called her over. He had planned to wait one more day, until Christmas Eve, but he was afraid their time together would be lost in the arrival of company. Alison would be coming in the afternoon and John in the morning. A big family dinner was planned.

He checked himself in the hall mirror as he passed. Wearing the red sweater she liked, new khakis, and Christmas socks, he smiled at his reflection. "Lookin' good," he said as he reached for the phone and dialed her number. Grace answered.

"Hi, Noah. Yes, she's right here, but there may be a change in plans."

"What do you mean? I've got everything all set up."

"Well-l-l," Grace drawled, "you talk to her."

There was a pause and some rustling in the background. "Heddo, Noah."

"Hi, darling. I've got dinner in the oven, the tree plugged in, and Christmas music playing in the background. Come on over," he said huskily.

"I can't, honey. I hab a code."

"A code .. er.. cold? When did you take that?"

"I woke up with it dis morning. Just a little sore throat yesterday. Then dis morning—wham!"

"Oh, I'm so sorry. Come on over, and I'll wrap you up in front of the fire and hand feed you."

"I don't want to gib it to you. And my head is so stuffy; I wouldn't be good company."

He hesitated. All the opportunities that he had to propose were foiled by one thing or another. It was worth risking a cold; he was tired of delays. "I'm not afraid. Come on and let Dr. Noah make you feel better."

"I look awful."

"You're always beautiful to me."

"Okay. I hobe you're not sorry."

He went to the hall closet and got out a fleece throw and pillow, then poured two glasses of wine and waited for her to knock. But she didn't knock, she just opened the door, slammed it, and stood there shivering. She smiled at him weakly, her nose red and swollen, her red curls damp and sticking up like steel wool, wearing faded blue sweats and socks under fleece lined buckskin slippers. Noah did a double take.

"I tode you I look horrible," she said defensively.

"Come here." He crossed over and took her into his arms. She nestled close with her head averted so as not to infect him. Pulling back and turning, she let out a sneeze, scrambling to cover her mouth with a ratty tissue.

He took her to the sofa and covered her with the throw. She leaned back against the downy pillow. "Dis is nice, honey, oh, just a min…" Another sneeze. "Sorry. Your tree looks so good, and the candles probably smell good, but I can't smell."

He handed her a glass, but she waved it away. "Habe you got orange juice? I'm afraid to drink that with all the antihistamines I hab in me. But you go ahead." She ran her fingers through her hair, aware that he looked particularly handsome, and she looked like a hag. "Did you do all dis for me? I missed you. I'm so glad you're back home." She reached for his hand.

He knelt down beside the sofa. "I'm so sorry you're sick. I shouldn't have insisted that you come over, feeling like you do."

"You're scared of my germs now." She drew back.

"No, honey. I had a lovely evening planned, but if you aren't up to it…"

"What's in the oven? I think I see smoke…" About that time, the alarm went off, blaring in their ears. He jumped up, bumping his knee on the coffee table, nearly capsizing the candles, and turned off the alarm. Limping and muttering under his breath, he took the charred Chinese food from the hot oven, yelling as he burnt his finger. Soot from the burned paper containers sifted over the floor. He threw the cartons in the sink and turned water on them, raising steam and more burnt aroma. Opening the window, he hurried to shut the kitchen door to contain the smell.

He rubbed his sore knee as he returned to Ginny. "Sorry about that. I thought I had the oven on warm. How do you feel about really having pizza for dinner?"

"I'm not hungry, Noah. Don't worry about it." She paused. "Do you habe any cereal?"

"Cereal?"

"Yeah, that sounds good to me."

"What a romantic dinner," he mumbled as he ventured back into the smoky kitchen and fixed two bowls of cereal. She gobbled hers down in a hurry.

"Dat's the only thing that has tasted good to me," she said as she handed him her empty bowl. "Tank you, sweetie. You dropped something under the table when you hit your knee." She squinted her eyes. "It looks like a ring."

He got down on his knees, painfully, and reached for the ring, sighing. The atmosphere for romance was definitely gone. But so what? It was now or never. He reached for her hand.

"Ginny, I meant for this to be a romantic evening."

"And I messed it up with this stupid code," she sniffed.

"And I practically set the house on fire. But forget that. This, my darling, is an engagement ring. It was Mom's. She wanted me to give it to you; she knew we were meant for each other from the very start. I want to ask you if you'll wear it for the rest of your life. I love you, Ginny. Will you marry me?"

Tears filled her red-rimmed eyes, and she was speechless as he slipped the antique diamond on her finger. She held her hand up to watch the sparkle of the stone in the candlelight. "Oh, it's beautiful. I lub it. And, yes, I will marry you, Noah. I lub you with all my heart. But don't kiss me. Just hold me."

He put his arms around her and snuggled down on the sofa beside her. As they kept their faces averted from each other, he began to chuckle.

"What's so funny?"

"This whole evening. What a mess. The only good thing about it was that you said 'yes'.

"Of course, I said 'yes'. If you could stand to look at me like dis and still propose, what else could I say? And tink of the story we can tell our grandchildren."

They laughed together and talked of wedding plans as the roaring fire in the fireplace burned down to embers, and the candles flickered every time Ginny sneezed.

Chapter 28

"I know I'm late," Alison grumbled to Grace as she pushed through the door, her arms loaded down with packages. "The traffic was terrible, and I had to stop for a wreck up ahead. I felt so sorry for those people, having an accident on Christmas Eve. Thank goodness, they didn't appear to be hurt badly." She dumped her packages under the tree and rose to give Grace a big hug. "Merry Christmas, Grace. Where's Ginny?"

"Merry Christmas, honey. She's upstairs in bed."

"What's wrong?"

"She has a cold, but she's much better today. I talked her into having a nap so she would feel good for dinner." She pulled at Alison's arm as she started for Ginny's bedroom. "Hey, don't go wake her up yet. Let her rest."

Alison arranged the pile of gifts around the tree and slowly touched the ornaments that Ginny had made though the years. Construction paper stars covered with glitter, colored Santa faces with cotton beards, and clothespin reindeer hung in harmony with shiny new glass balls. They had saved every one, she and Laura Belle, even though Ginny wanted to throw them out for more glamorous decorations when she was a teenager.

"This tree IS Christmas for me," she said to Grace.

"It's beautiful. Lots of memories there. Now, how about some fresh coffee?"

"Oh, it smells heavenly," Alison said as she followed Grace into the kitchen. The aroma of the turkey and dressing mingled with the cinnamony smell of apple cake and hazelnut coffee. As they filled their cups, John came in the back door with a small bag.

"Hi, Alison," he said with a smile before turning toward Grace. "Are these the right kind of candles? It's all they had left."

"They'll do nicely. Now hang up your coat and have coffee with Alison in the living room while I finish up here."

"Let me help," Alison protested. "You've done too much."

"No, I haven't. Ginny made some of the casseroles and the cake and froze them last week. I just did the turkey and dressing. So scoot! Get out of my hair!"

They took their coffee to the living room and settled in front of the fire. "I'm glad it's cold," Alison remarked. "Some of our Christmases are so warm that it doesn't seem like Christmas."

"Yeah, having a fire in the fireplace makes it complete, even if it is gas logs." As they watched the flickering flames, he added, "Ginny is so fortunate to have Grace. She's like a mother hen."

"She always was. Grace and her husband had no children, and they adored Ginny. He died when Ginny was about ten, and it broke her heart."

"She lost both father figures in a short time," he mused, thinking of Alison's father's premature death.

Just then, Noah exploded through the front door. "Merry Christmas, everybody." He set a box of gifts by the tree and shook John's hand, then gave Alison a hug.

"Where's our girl?" he called as he hung his coat on the hall tree.

"Napping. Grace said she had a cold."

He grinned. "Yeah, I know. Think I'll go and see if I can help Grace." He escaped quickly to the kitchen.

"She won't let you," Alison called, then stood, reaching her hand to John. "Let's set the table. At least we can do that much."

The dining room table was already covered with the special red tablecloth. Simple greenery and candles filled the center. Alison handed silverware to John, and he followed her around as she positioned the china and napkins.

"This china belonged to my great-grandmother," she told him as she ran a finger around the golden rim of a plate. "It's so delicate we only use it for special occasions. As you can see, each place setting is a little different. And she painted it all herself. That amazes me."

"Young ladies painted china back in that era, didn't they? It's gorgeous. I promise to be careful, although I'd be more comfortable if it were plastic."

She laughed. "We've broken a few pieces, but we don't cry over it. When it's gone, it's gone. But it is special."

"Oh, here you are. Look at the pretty table," Ginny said from the doorway. She gave her mother a kiss and John a hug. "Merry Christmas," she whispered to both. In her bright green sweater and slacks, her red hair shining, she looked anything but sick.

"So you're better? Grace said you've been sick."

"She gave me some super duper decongestant, and I'm not as bad as I was yesterday. Bless Grace. She has been so good to me, Mom. I don't believe I could have stood up and labored over that turkey and dressing."

Grace came into the room bearing the cake to sit on the side board. "Well, it's ready. Now you can help."

They loaded the table with turkey, casseroles, dressing and vegetables. Alison lit the candles and smiled at John. "Would you say grace for us?"

He bowed his head and began. "Lord, we give you thanks for this special time, for this bounty, and for the love that surrounds this table. We are blessed beyond measure. As we feast, grant us mercy and forgiveness and keep us in your care. Amen."

"Thank you, John," Noah said softly. "Before we start, I have something to say. You know that I've come to love your beautiful daughter very much. And she loves me, too, why I can't imagine." He laughed a little nervously, as everyone waited, smiling. "Uh–I have a question. Alison and John, I have asked your daughter to be my wife, and she said 'yes'. We would like your blessing." He paused and added, hopefully, "Do we have it?"

"Oh, my," Alison gasped, looking at John. "Of course, we give our blessing, don't we?" She and John went around the table to hug Ginny and Noah. Ginny beamed and held out her hand. She had kept her diamond turned inward so no one would guess too soon.

"Oh, the ring is beautiful," Alison murmured as though she hadn't seen it before. "Welcome to the family, Noah." She brushed away a happy tear as she kissed them both.

"I've felt like a member of this family from the first day I met Ginny," he said as they sat back down. From her place, Grace just smiled.

"You knew about this already, didn't you?" Alison said, pointing her finger at her dear friend.

"I set it all up," she bragged. "Or did the best I could to help it along, anyway. Then Ginny came down with the sniffles. But it all worked out fine."

As Alison watched her daughter lean over to kiss her new fiancé, she felt a mixture of joy for their approaching marriage and sadness for something she couldn't put her finger on. John was looking at her with so much hope in his eyes that when she turned to smile at him, she quickly tore her gaze away, realizing what the touch of sadness in her heart was all about.

"So much for that," Grace said, abruptly. "The food's getting cold. John, please carve the turkey so we can start." The clatter of silverware against china and the hum of appreciation as the food was passed made a joyful noise that filled the old house that Christmas Eve.

Chapter 29

The New Year blew in with snowy weather, perfect for making wedding plans before a fire. Ginny wanted a small wedding at home, and Noah was happy that it would be a simple affair. It was understood, without any discussion, that they would live in Ginny's house and keep it in the family.

She grew more excited as the days passed and began the search for just the right dress. She shopped with Grace and with Alison, but failed to find anything that suited her. Finally, her mother informed her that time was running out, and she must come to a decision. An early March weekend found them in the city, hitting the shops.

"Well, Ginny Lee, turn around so ah can get a better look. Oh, beautiful, beautiful." Lee-Ann Grooms smiled at her cousin, twirling around in the white strapless wedding dress with tiers of ruffles. "That's my favorite so far. What do you think, Aunt Alison?"

Alison crossed her legs and leaned forward in her chair. "Hmmm. It's a lovely dress, but..."

"It's not for me, too much fru fru." Ginny batted down the full skirt. "I feel like Scarlett returning to Tara. Let me see the simplest thing you have," she said, turning to the saleslady.

"Dear, we have the most delightful off-white..." the tiny lady began as she propelled Ginny with a dainty hand.

"But I wanted white-white," Ginny protested as she was led back to the dressing room.

"Mercy!" Lee-Ann exclaimed. "Ah hope this is the last store for today. Your child is wearing me out! Ah am ready for a big latte. Was ah this hard to please last yeah?" She was referring to her own wedding the previous June. Ginny had been her bridesmaid and, in turn, had asked Lee-Ann to be her matron-of-honor.

Alison put her hand to her aching back and stretched. It had been a long day. She and Ginny had driven to Nashville, picked up Lee-Ann, and hit the bridal dress trail. She, too, was ready for coffee and a side of beef to go with it. Nodding her head in answer to Lee-Ann's question, she thought back to past days when she had accompanied Lee-Ann and her mother, Gloria, on these rounds.

"I'm sorry Gloria couldn't come with us."

"Well, she just doesn't feel like herself yet. She did fine after her surgery, but it's just taking longer to get her energy back than she expected."

"Ginny and I will run by and see her before we head home. I've got a book for her that I just know she'll love. It's called People of the Land. I met Beth Daniel, the author, at a book signing and had her sign one just for Gloria."

Actually Gloria was Alison's first cousin, but they had been as close growing up as sisters, and their daughters always referred to them as 'Aunt Gloria' and 'Aunt Alison'. Like Ginny, Lee-Ann had been an only child, and until her parents moved to Nashville when the girls were in college, the two were as close as their mothers had been.

Alison smiled at Lee-Ann as she remembered her wedding the year before—a big, ornate, glamorous occasion–and wished Ginny would have planned a more formal wedding. But she had her heart set on a simple ceremony at home with just friends and family.

Closing her eyes, Alison envisioned the church decorated in greenery and white blossoms. As the big doors opened, she could see Ginny sweeping through in a bouffant gown with a long train and veil, gliding down the church isle on John's arm. John's arm! She opened her eyes with a start. Everyone in the church would wonder who John was and remember that Ginny's father was supposed to be dead. Why hadn't that occurred to her before?

"That must be why Ginny was so insistent on a home wedding," she murmured aloud. Then hearing Lee-Ann gasp, she turned her eyes toward her daughter moving slowly toward them. She was radiant in a long white silk sheath with a mandarin collar, embroidered all over with just the palest tint of pink and silver threads woven through the design. The headdress was a simple matching coronet with veiling that slipped under Ginny's upswept hair and draped almost to the hem. The effect was shimmering with elegance.

"That's it!" Lee-Ann sprung up and clasped her hands. "It's you! It doesn't show enough skin to be in style, but that's your choice. After all you don't have my bust."

Ginny's eyes sparkled as she turned to her mother. Alison was speechless; she had never seen Ginny look so beautiful. Her eyes filled with tears as she went to her daughter and took her by the hands. "I love it," was all she could say.

"It's just what I was looking for," Ginny said softly as she ran her fingers down the lustrous fabric. She pressed her stomach in as she viewed the dress from the side. "And I'll have to lose five pounds right here."

"Okay. Pin it, tuck it, whatever you need to do," Lee-Ann said crisply to the saleslady, then whimpered pitifully to her cousin. "Ginny, honey, we're starving. It's three o'clock in the afternoon. Have mercy!"

"Okay, I'll be back in a jif." Ginny turned, humming the wedding march and throwing kisses over her shoulder.

Lee-Ann rolled her big brown eyes and complained in her thick southern drawl. "She's not even crabby, and ah feel like ah might just collapse right heah and eat the arm off this sofa."

After her fitting, the three women finally sat down to a very late lunch at a tearoom close to the bridal shop, too tired to go any further. Alison and Lee-Ann wolfed down their spinach salads while Ginny picked at hers.

"What's wrong, honey?" Aren't you hungry?" Alison said with her mouth full.

"I'm too excited, I guess. I keep thinking that I'd like to rush home and show this dress to Noah."

"Horrors! You know you can't do that. He'll see you soon enough. After all, heah it is March, and you've just now bought the dress. Now we have to come up with somethin' for me in pink. Pink! Ugh!" Lee-Ann popped another dainty cake in her mouth and shivered with delight at the taste of the chocolate confection.

"Well, of course I wouldn't show him the dress, silly. I said that's what I'd like to do. And you look good in pink, very pale pink with your gorgeous black hair. You'll be beautiful."

"Naturally, I we-ell," Lee-Ann agreed in her very best Scarlett O'Hara imitation, smoothing down her wavy hair, and they all laughed—blood sugar and good humor restored.

Ginny had never been so happy in her life. In less than three months, she would marry Noah in her own living room with everyone she loved around her. She wished she could wave a magic wand and make the time fly by faster; she could hardly wait for her wedding day.

Chapter 30

At the little cafe around the corner from her apartment, Alison sat sipping on her second cup of coffee. The early morning traffic moved slowly as small business owners and apartment dwellers up and down the street stopped by for their first caffeine fix. She tilted her head back to let the sun warm her face. This had become her favorite place for breakfast on Saturdays, but it was her first time this year to sit out on the sidewalk and watch the neighborhood wake up.

She reached for her opened book and tried again to focus on finding her place.

"Read that one, and that one...can't remember where I stopped," she mumbled to herself. With a sigh she put it back down and leaned on the table, chin cradled in her hands. Her mind wandered to the upcoming wedding.

Ginny had done so much of the hard work, and Alison felt stirrings of guilt about not going down today to help with the little chores. But Lee-Ann and her husband, Cliff, had spent the night at Ginny's last night and were leaving out early for a golf tournament that he was playing in. Then John was driving down later on.

The breeze ruffled her hair, and she pulled her light sweater more tightly around her. Ginny's father came unbidden to her mind, as he so often did. Lately, she had deliberately stayed away from Ginny's whenever he was going to be there. She knew he hoped for more than just the new friendship they had forged with each other. But she couldn't help the memories of pain and loneliness that crept into her head whenever she thought of turning to him, of confessing her own strong feelings. She would stay away until the last minute preparations for the wedding. That would give them a cooling off period. Then, maybe, he could see more plainly that there was too much baggage from both sides to begin a relationship other than being parents to Ginny.

She paid her bill and walked slowly to her apartment. Around the old brick homes and the new condos the bright yellow forsythias bushes had faded, leaving yellow petals scattered on the ground. But tulips were popping up everywhere, their many colored blooms bobbing in the breeze. The grass was s shimmering bright green, and the sky a brilliant blue. She felt a pang of regret that she had chosen to stay home this weekend, this absolutely gorgeous weekend. Going back to her empty apartment felt like going back to prison.

As she approached the building, an ambulance was pulling away, its siren blaring. Hurrying up to the group of renters who had come outside, she asked, "What's happened. Is someone ill?"

Her down-the-hall neighbor, Mrs. Wheeler, shook her head, sadly. "It's Nora Keane. I took her some of my hot muffins and found her lying on the floor. I think she may have had a stroke."

"Oh, no," Alison said, clutching her book to her chest. "Not Mrs. Keane. She's so bouncy and full of energy, so kind to everyone."

"I know. She thought a lot of you. Talked about how worried she was about your daughter and all. Listen, would you mind going back to her apartment with me and helping to tidy up a bit? She knocked over something when she fell, and there's glass all over."

She followed Mrs. Wheeler into Mrs. Keane's kitchen, and together they cleaned up glass and washed up dishes. Alison went into the small living room and bent to fold up an afghan lying on the floor. As she did, a picture fell out on the rug. Mrs. Wheeler made a tsk tsk sound.

"I bet she was moping over that picture again."

"Who is this?" Alison asked, looking at a very young, handsome man in a military uniform.

"Oh, that's Roger—can't remember his last name. Anyway, he was her first love, way before she married Mr. Keane. He dumped her for another girl, I believe. Then, after Mr. Keane passed years ago, Roger came back into her life. But she'd have no part of him. He died suddenly a few months ago. Poor Nora was just heartbroken that she hadn't taken him back. They should've had years together. She just couldn't get over his death."

"She never told me any of this. Of course, we didn't get to talk that much with me working and going back and forth to Ginny's."

"No, Nora's a wonderful person, but she kept her business to herself. The only reason I knew was because Nora and I have been friends for forty years."

As they finished up and were leaving the apartment, Mrs. Wheeler patted her hand. "Don't you worry now. Nora Keane is one tough woman. I'll call you when I check on her. Write down your number for me."

Alison returned to her small rooms more depressed than ever. She thought about Mrs. Keane all day, remembering how kind she was to look after Monroe for so long and refusing to take a cent for it. Giving up on getting any cleaning done, Alison wrote letters and paid bills. About four o'clock, she settled down with the book and managed to get a few pages behind her when the phone rang. It was Mrs. Wheeler.

"Alison, dear? I'm calling from the hospital. I have some bad news. Nora passed away about an hour ago. The stroke was massive, and there wasn't anything more they could do. I knew you'd want to know." Her voice trembled as she relayed the news.

"I'm so sorry," Alison mumbled.

"Dear, if you have time, would you mind fixing a dish—anything you have on hand. The family will be coming in, and I thought it would be nice if the neighbors had a meal for them. What do you think about lunch for tomorrow?"

"Oh, of course. I have the makings of a chicken casserole, so I'll fix that. And thank you, Mrs. Wheeler, for calling and letting me know."

She reached for Monroe, who was lying at her feet, and carried him in her arms to the back door and looked out. Beyond the pale cityscape, the sun was dropping on the horizon, sinking into shades of mauve and pink. Feeling sad at the loss, she wondered if Nora Keane had forgiven Roger before he died. She hoped that she had. Putting her chin on Monroe's soft head, she felt the tears form in the back of her eyes.

"Have I really forgiven John?" she asked, softly.

Monroe licked her face and rubbed his soft nose against her wet cheek.

Chapter 31

Two weeks before the wedding, John picked Alison up and drove down to help Ginny and Noah do a little work on the house. Alison was so excited to see him. It had seemed a long time since they had been together. She found herself talking non stop and laughing at every little thing, but John, for the most part, seemed deep in thought during their drive. She felt a little disappointed at the distance he seemed to be putting between them. Perhaps he had changed his mind about renewing their relationship. The thought made her grow silent as they drew closer to the house.

They found Ginny and Noah cleaning the dining room rug. After a brief greeting, they got their assignments from the bride-to-be and fell to work. Alison took down the sheers in the living room to wash, taking time to mend a torn hem. While they washed, she dragged out the vacuum and went over the furniture and baseboards throughout the downstairs. John had just finished painting the porch furniture when the sudden rain shower moved in from the west and drove him inside.

Now he stood at the window watching the billowy sheets of rain drift like a curtain across the lawn. Lost in thoughts of the past few months, he felt as dejected as the peonies that were bending to the ground, their petals torn by the wind. He had spent as much time as the winter weather allowed with Ginny. But most of the time, Alison stayed away when he was there. His time with her had been limited since Christmas, and he felt that he was losing the closeness that was developing between them. He had looked forward so much to this trip to spend a little time with her.

Alison entered from the dining room carrying a tray of coffee and cookies. Setting it on the coffee table, she paused to admire the figure in the window, the strong arms on the window frame, muscular in an old work shirt with rolled up sleeves. He was still as slim as when they first met. She cleared her throat, but he didn't turn.

"Here's coffee."

He jerked around with a smile. "Sorry, I didn't hear you come in. That does smell good." He sat on the sofa and took the cup from her. She seated herself across from him in the faded red silk chair.

"What's next on the list?" he asked as he shook his head when offered a cookie.

"The guest bath, whenever Ginny and Noah get back with the wallpaper. Thank goodness they pulled off the old paper so we don't have to do that." Alison leaned back and took a sip of her coffee. She was already tired, but it was a good tired. She loved to paint and fix up this old house, and she wanted it to look especially pretty for the wedding in two weeks. Shaking her head at John as he pushed the cookie plate toward her, she grinned. "Ginny and I are trying to lose five pounds. She made it, I haven't!"

"You don't need to lose even one pound," John told her with admiration in his eyes. "You're perfect just like you are."

She blushed and smiled her thanks. "You're lucky. You're naturally slim. Must have been in your genes. My mother got pretty chubby as she got older—or at least before she got sick."

"Well, you're far from chubby. You haven't really changed that much from college days."

For the first time, she didn't flinch at his mention of that time. The space she had put between herself and John had caused her to reflect long and hard on their relationship. Ever since her neighbor's death, she had focused on forgiveness. The more she thought of the past, the more she realized that he had almost as much forgiving to do as she did. He had tried to make amends at every turn. She had accepted and promptly rejected his attempts to make up for his mistake.

Now here, in the midst of the chaos of the wedding, she felt peaceful when John was near, even when he mentioned their past. The anger that lurked in the corners of her mind was gone. When she agreed to their driving down together, she was excited. And as she looked into his green eyes, she suddenly realized why. It wasn't just the excitement of the wedding. It was simply being with him. The fear had finally deserted her, that old fear of being hurt again. She looked at him and sighed deeply, feeling a lightness of spirit that she hadn't felt before.

"Did I say something wrong?"

"Sorry, I didn't mean to stare. I just realized something, John. This feels perfectly natural to me, the two of us sitting here drinking coffee, working on this house together. There's no longer a knot in my chest because the wrong things might be said. It's...it's comfortable, don't you think?"

He was so surprised that he almost asked her to repeat it. He wanted to pull her up from the chair and kiss her. But instead he basked in the happiness that spread through his whole body.

"It's taken us a year," he murmured softly, "but that's okay. I'm glad you feel relaxed about our relationship. I wouldn't blame you if you never reached this stage after what I put you through."

"Shhh," she touched her lips with her finger. "Let's talk about now, not..."

The stamping of feet in the hall interrupted her, and he swallowed his disappointment at the intrusion. Noah and Ginny came in after hanging up their wet raincoats on the hall tree.

"What a messy day." Ginny flung herself down beside John, then cocked her head to one side. "Are you okay, John? You look kinda pale."

"Just a little indigestion or something. Could we turn on the gas logs? It's chilly in here. Can't believe it's almost May." He felt a sudden chill.

Alison turned on the logs although it seemed warm in the room to her. "This is blackberry winter, so Grace says. It'll be warm again in a day or two. Want some coffee, you two?"

"I'll get it." Noah went into the kitchen and came back with two cups. "We got the wallpaper," he said, handing Ginny her cup.

Alison brought the package in from the hall and pulled out a roll. "Oh, it's beautiful. And I love this border. As soon as you rest a bit, we'll get the ladders and start on this before dinner."

Soon they were at work hanging the new paper. Although the guest bath was large, there was only room for three to work comfortably around the ladder, so Alison went into the kitchen and began preparing salad and spaghetti sauce for their dinner. Grover, lying placidly by the back door, raised his head and opened one eye, then dropped his head between his paws.

She talked to him as though he was another adult while she put together the salad and browned the beef for the sauce. His fluffy tail thumped on the floor with every word. Finally he rose and whined to be let out. "You get no peace, huh, boy? Bet you won't stay out very long in this wind." She let him out through the back porch and continued her chore. She had the meal almost completed when Ginny came into the kitchen.

"Mom, come here."

Alison dried her hands on the towel. "Are you through already?"

"No, it's John. He's not feeling well. We made him lie down on the guest bed. He's really nauseous." They hurried to the bedroom where John laid, his face pinched and white.

Alison sat on the bed and touched his forehead. "What's wrong? Are you in pain?"

He patted her hand. "It's probably nothing. I didn't feel very good this morning. I've had some pain in my chest and stomach—thought it was something I ate last night."

"Where are you hurting right now?' Noah asked bending over the other side of the bed.

John moved his hands over his chest. "All over here. It's gotten increasing worse, and when I started reaching up to put on the wallpaper, I got really sick and dizzy."

"We should get you to the emergency room," Alison said, jumping up.

"Give me a few minutes. Maybe it'll go away." Even as he spoke, he sucked in his breath with pain.

Heart! That word was running through Ginny's mind. She looked at her mother's shocked face and pulled her out into the hall.

"You're right, Mom. We need to get him to the hospital. If it is his heart, we can't waste any time."

"Heart? You think it's his heart?" Alison felt cold fear wash through her veins. She raced to the phone and dialed 911.

The ambulance was there in five minutes. John no longer protested as they loaded him. Alison climbed in to ride with him, but the emergence personnel seated her out of their way as they checked John out.

"You'll be okay, John. It may just be something…"

He interrupted her with a moan. "Stay with me, okay?"

She reached past the attendant and squeezed his hand. "I'm right here. You just try to relax and breathe like they told you."

Even though the hospital was close by, the ride seemed long to Alison. As they wheeled John into the emergency room, Ginny and Noah were right behind. They all went into the cubicle with him but were soon asked to leave.

"If you'll go down to the waiting room, we'll come to you just as soon as we do an evaluation," the nurse said gently.

Numbly, they walked down the hall. Alison's hands were shaking as she lowered herself into a chair. With tears seeping through her eyelids, she murmured, "Please, please don't let it be a heart attack." Ginny threaded her fingers through her mother's and held her hands still. Even though she was anxious and worried, she was surprised at her mother's emotional reaction.

"All we can do now is wait, Mom," she said gently. They both looked up at the clock at the same time.

Chapter 32

A smiling white-haired doctor in surgical garb appeared in the waiting room, startling them with his booming voice. "Are you waiting for word on Mr. Fredericks?" They rose, but he motioned them to sit as he took a chair and turned it around to face them.

Alison felt her knees begin to shake. She willed her hands to stay still in her lap and tried to clear her mind as the doctor began to speak.

"This is a classic gall bladder attack. He says he's had them off and on for a year and just thought it was something that didn't agree with him. We're going to run some tests to see where the gallstones are. If the duct is clear, it's a simple procedure. If it's not, we may have to either let the stones pass or do the old fashioned operation where we have to open him up. We'll know after these tests and let you know. He says he hasn't eaten, is that right?"

"Not that I know of," Alison replied. "We were so afraid that it was his heart." She breathed an audible sigh of relief.

"His heart is fine. Ordinarily, I'd rather wait and let him get back to his own doctor, but I'm a little concerned about pancreatitis setting in as he's in quite a lot of pain now. So sit tight. We'll let you know shortly."

Alison and Ginny put their arms around each other in relief. After reporting to Grace and waiting through numerous cups of coffee, they heard the test results from the doctor.

"Everything looks good for surgery, and I think it best to get this over with. He doesn't want to put it off either," he said. "If you'll stand outside, they'll roll him right by here on the way to surgery. Don't worry. He'll be okay."

They stood in the doorway, and soon the gurney came up the hall, the rubber wheels making a soft rhythm on the tiled floor. Alison, Ginny, and Noah met and walked along beside it as the nurses moved toward the big double doors marked surgery, then stopped.

Ginny leaned over her father's chalk white face. "John, everything's going to be fine. We'll be right here waiting. You just relax. Remember how you took care of me? Well, we're going to take care of you this time." She felt tears forming in the corners of her eyes as she remembered the days of her recuperation at John's cottage.

He smiled, obviously a little groggy already. He loosened his hands from the blanket and wiggled his fingers toward Alison. She grasped his hand, cold with dread, and held it to her cheek. "You're going to be fine.

The doctor said so. I will not leave as long as you're here. There's so much…"

"Gotta move on," the nurse tucked John's hand back in its place and hit the button to throw open the big doors that quickly closed behind them. Alison stared at them as if they would open again and bring him back out.

Noah took Ginny's hand. "I don't know about you girls, but I seem to remember missing a good dinner somewhere back there. How about we go to the cafeteria before they close and get a bite?"

"Good idea. Mom, you'll come, too, won't you? It'll be a while before they come and tell us anything."

Alison nodded and followed them into the elevator. Food was the last thing on her mind, but since she had already determined to stay with John when he got out of surgery, she knew she should have something to tide her over.

"This is slim pickins'," Ginny murmured as they looked around the cafeteria. The hot bar was being cleaned, but the salad bar was still open and a few pieces of dessert still remained, so the three took salads and pie and settled at a table. Alison nibbled as Ginny and Noah ate hungrily. Noting Alison's far away expression; Ginny put her fork down and patted her mother's hand.

"He'll be fine, Mom. Aren't you glad it was just his gall bladder and not his heart?"

"You bet," Alison answered quickly. "But he may be pretty sick for a little while when he first gets out of surgery. I'm going to stay, but you both go home. If he's doing okay and sleeping, I may come home later."

Ginny nodded. She was a little surprised at the depth of her mother's concern for John. It seemed to go beyond their newly found friendly relationship. This pretty much confirmed the hunch that she had entertained in the back of her mind that her mother was still in love and had been for a long time.

Later, back in the waiting room, the surgeon returned to tell them that all went well. They didn't have to do the radical surgery, so John just had tiny incisions and was already beginning to wake up in recovery. They went up to the room number he gave them and waited for John to be delivered. In less than an hour, an alert John was tucked into his bed, IVs checked, and vitals taken.

As the room emptied of nurses, John turned his head to look at them all. "Now, I'm fine, and you don't have to stay. The nurse told me that I can have pain medication whenever I want. Right now, I feel drowsy and relieved that it's over. I'll probably sleep like a log," he assured them with a thick tongue.

"Noah and Ginny are going home, but I'm staying. No, don't shake your head, I'm staying. At least until you go off to dreamland."

He grinned and motioned for Ginny to give him a kiss on the cheek. "Your mother has spoken, so I guess we'll have to humor her. Thanks for being here for me, Ginny, Noah. You go home and rest. You've got two weeks until the wedding, and they'll be very busy days."

Ginny kissed him and Noah shook his hand. "I'll take your girl home then. Have a good night, John."

"Mom, call me if you need anything, hear?"

Alison shook her head. "'Night. I'll be in when I get there. If Grace's light is still on, give her a call and tell her how John is." She waved them off down the hall and turned back to the patient.

"Water?" He tried to moisten his lips with a dry tongue.

"Not until the nurse says its okay. Just chips for now," Alison spooned ice chips into his mouth, and he savored them. She took away the ice and tucked the blanket under his feet, making him comfortable. He patted the bed, and she pulled up her chair and laid her head down on the mattress.

"You scared me," she mumbled into the bed.

"What?" he asked as he reached over to gently push the dark curls out of her face.

She took his hand in both of hers. "You scared me. I was so afraid it was your heart. I was afraid I might lose you, and I don't know what I would have done." He tried to rise up to look at her, but she eased him down. "No, no, don't move. Just rest, and I'll be quiet."

"I don't want you to be quiet," he said, shaking his head vigorously. "Keep on talking. This is the best conversation we've ever had."

She laughed. "I have you trapped now, don't I? You have to listen to my every word. Okay, here goes." She took a deep breath. "I...I love you, John. I don't think I ever really stopped. You know I fought it hard, I really did. But when I thought you might be taken away from me, I knew I would be sick with regrets if that happened. You have tried to atone for your mistakes, but I just held on to my anger. Why did I do that? We're different people now, and we've been through a lot. We deserve to be together and put the past behind us. Do you think we can do that?" Her voice lowered to a mere whisper.

"This is the best moment of my life," he said with a grimace as he tried to reach for her with both arms. She carefully leaned over him, avoiding the tubes, and kissed his dry lips, his forehead, and his neck as she snuggled her face in his shoulder.

"I never thought I'd hear those words. Oh, Alison, I love you so much. I have always loved you, always. Thank you, thank you, sweetheart. You've made my dreams come true. We can make it, I know we can." She kissed him again, then pulled herself up as a nurse came in to check him.

"Why aren't you asleep?" She frowned but with a twinkle in her blue eyes. "All this kissing can wait until you've had a little sleep. I'm going to give you a shot to help you rest."

"Please, no," he begged. "I don't want to sleep now, really. I feel great—wonderful, in fact! Don't give me that stuff!"

She ignored him as she shot the medication into his IV. "Oh, you'll thank me for this later when the feeling comes back and you're whining." She winked at Allison and added. "I think she'll be here when you wake up. Am I right?"

"Absolutely," Alison answered. "Shut your eyes and give in to it, John. We'll talk more in the morning." She kissed his forehead and whispered, "I do love you."

He closed his eyes. "Best day of my life," he said as the drugs began coursing through his veins.

When the nurse left the room, Alison dropped her head on the bed rail, whispering, "Thank you, God. And thank you, too, Mrs. Keane."

Chapter 33

Ginny rolled over and looked at the luminous dial—five o'clock. Through the crack in the blinds, she could see the faintest light of early morning. She jumped up and opened them to see if the sky was clear. A few pale stars still twinkled, and the fading moon still cast its shadow even as the darkness lifted like fog.

"Yes!" she exclaimed as she flopped backwards on her bed. It was her wedding day and, although the weather report said 'clear and dry', she was delighted to see the cloudless sky. "'Happy is the bride the sun shines on'," she repeated the old adage to herself, hugging herself with delight.

She had slept little, waking up off and on, too excited to stay asleep. Her wedding dress and veil hung from the closet door frame, her shoes underneath, ready to step into. Her bag was open on the chest at the foot of the bed, packed except for her cosmetics.

A delicious thrill ran through her as she thought of their honey moon on the coast. Their longing for each other had been so intense the past few weeks, but she insisted—and Noah had reluctantly agreed—that they would wait until their honeymoon. Even though it was considered old-fashioned anymore to observe restraints, they were both raised with those kinds of values. It was part of their faith.

The smell of coffee brewing interrupted her sweet, torrid thoughts. Slipping into her robe, she walked bare-foot to the kitchen where she found her mother sitting at the small table with a steaming cup in front of her.

"Good morning. What are you doing up so early?" She reached for a cup and poured it full, breathing the aroma.

Alison ran her fingers through her mussed hair. "I woke up an hour ago and couldn't go back to sleep. This is the first time I've been the mother of the bride, you know. Big day in my life! How about you? Did you sleep at all?"

Ginny's hand drifted lightly over her mother's shoulders as she took a chair next to her. "I dozed rather than slept. Kept waking up and looking at the clock. Noah probably slept like a log," she said with a laugh. "Want me to fix us some eggs and bacon?"

"I'm not that hungry. But last night I ran by the store after rehearsal and picked us up some of those sinfully delicious Danish that you love and some fresh squeezed orange juice. Maybe Lee-Ann will wake up and join us."

"You're the best mom I ever had! And you know perfectly well that Lee-Ann will sleep as late as possible, which means more for us." Ginny grinned at Alison as she warmed the pastries in the microwave and poured juice. "This is our last chance to just sit and talk before I'm a married woman. Is there anything special you'd like to talk about?" The grin turned wicked as she cocked her head with one eyebrow raised.

Alison laughed. "Whatever you're getting at, I think we'd better stick to the plans for today. And anyway, you're being paged at the moment."

Grover whined from the back porch; Ginny let him in and poured dry dog food into his bowl. "Ole' buddy, you've got to stay out today. We don't need dog hair all over the place, even if you are freshly bathed and looking good." He swished his shaggy tail back and forth across the floor, sitting politely while she talked to him, his broad head cupped in her hands.

"You're sure John won't mind taking care of Grover while we're gone?"

Alison turned her head to hide her smile. "No, it was his idea. Besides Grace will take over when she gets back from visiting her friend later on."

"Speaking of John, he must really be sleeping soundly upstairs or he would be down for coffee. I can't believe he did so well after his surgery. He's an amazing physical specimen!" Ginny brought a scrap of paper from her robe pocket and began to rattle off chores.

After discussing the 'to do' list, they put it aside to do a little reminiscing about Ginny's childhood and teen-age years. Their laughter finally did wake John up, and he joined them at the table. Then Lee-Ann staggered downstairs like a zombie and reached for the coffee Alison poured for her.

After swigging down her first cup, she became alert. "That is the most wonderful bed, cousin. Thank you for not making me sleep on the couch, Aunt Alison. Ah'm sorry you had to. Did you get any sleep at all?" She stretched her long legs under the table.

"I slept fine until early morning. Then I just had to get up; I was too excited to stay there."

After awhile, they reluctantly left the cozy kitchen and got dressed for their assigned tasks. John ran last minute errands to the rental place for candelabras and to the grocery with Alison's list. Alison and Ginny put the finishing touches on the altar in front of the fireplace and added more lengths of tulle around the tall floor candles while Lee-Ann made beds and tidied the upstairs.

Later in the morning, the flowers were delivered and promptly refrigerated. Lee-Ann's parents, Gloria and Charles arrived. After a quick coffee break, Grace took them home with her to help assemble food for the reception. Lee-Ann joined Alison and Ginny at the beauty salon. Alison surprised them with facials and massages as well as having their hair and nails done. They came home looking beautiful and totally relaxed.

"Law, ah feel so gorgeous," Lee-Ann exclaimed as she turned in front of the hall mirror. "When ah get on that beautiful pink dress, nobody will even notice the bride." She wrinkled her nose at Ginny.

"You wish. You'll just fade into the wallpaper when I walk in, honey chile," Ginny mocked her cousin's accent.

Grace had fixed a paper plate lunch of chicken salad and fruit that they dove into eagerly. Across the street,

Noah, his aunt and uncle and his best man, Jerry, feasted on his Aunt Mary's fried chicken and potato salad. Neither Ginny nor Noah could eat much.

The hour was fast approaching. Ginny and Lee-Ann disappeared upstairs to finish Ginny's packing and get dressed. Alison helped Grace carry the remainder of the food from her house and arranged the table.

"It's perfect." Alison smoothed the organdy overlay one more time.

"Did you know Grover dug out of the back yard? I noticed the hole under the fence." Grace was pinning up one corner of the cloth with a beribboned daisy.

"That hound! Wonder where he went? Ginny will have a fit if anything happens to that dog. Of all days for him to go wandering! I'd better get John to help me hunt for him. If you don't mind, ask Gloria to help you with the punch."

"But you have to dress. We only have a little over an hour."

"Well, Ginny will be out in her wedding gown looking for him if I don't." She took off down the hall, calling for John.

The two of them set off in John's truck, slowly driving up and down the streets with the windows down, calling for Grover. Fifteen minutes passed, then twenty. Alison was beginning to panic when they spotted him at the park three blocks over. They stopped and called the big yellow dog that bolted toward them with his head down, looking dazed and confused. The closer he came, the more they realized that he had come in close contact with a skunk.

"Phew. That's awful." Alison exclaimed, trying to hold him as far away from her as she could. "What on earth are we going to do? The wedding is in less than forty-five minutes. We can't just leave him."

"Here, I'll tie him in the back of the truck." He looped a piece of rope through his collar and fastened it to the rail. "Get in. Hurry. Have you got any tomato juice in the house?"

"Grace put up gallons of it last summer. Is that good for skunk odor?"

"I've always heard that it is. You get the juice and the strongest soap you have, and I'll wash him outside."

They drove madly to the house and pulled the truck around to the back yard. Alison flew through Grace's back door and ran back with three quarts of tomatoes clutched to her chest.

"The juice is all gone. There's only tomatoes left," she said, panting.

"That'll have to do." John pushed the frightened dog in his tub and lathered him from head to tail. Then he poured the tomatoes and their juice over Grover, squashing them with his hands as he rubbed the red fruit into the poor dog's fur. Alison opened another jar, and together they scrubbed the terrified Grover with tomatoes, then soap again, and hosed him down. He howled in protest when the cold spray engulfed him. John dumped the tub of red, soapy, hairy mess while Alison hurriedly tied Grover to the fence. He shivered and shook, looking so forlorn that she had to feel sorry for the poor dog.

"What do you mean 'poor baby'? We smell almost as bad as he did. And we've got twenty minutes." John was not quite back to normal after his surgery and the bathing activity left him exhausted.

"Right!" She snapped to attention. "You shower at Grace's, and I'll send her over with your clothes. I'll shower upstairs. Use all the good smelling stuff she has."

They took off in a run. As Alison headed into the bathroom, Ginny came out into the hall. "Mom! What's that smell? It smells like…"

"It is. You can thank Grover for the aroma. Quick, get some scented candles and light them. I'll have to wash my hair, too. Oh, my lovely coif…wasted." She slammed the bathroom door.

"I can't believe this," Ginny complained. "Where is John?" she yelled through the door.

"Showering at Grace's. Send someone over with his tux." The noise of the shower blurred remains of her conversation.

"Grace?" A frantic Ginny ran down the stairs with Lee-Ann fluttering on her heels. "Help!"

Twenty minutes later, friends were crowded into the living room as the string quartet began to play–and play–and play.

Chapter 34

The altar before the fireplace was draped with ferns placed at varying heights. Tall candles flickered from the hearth and the windows as did the tapers on the mantel, anchored in a garland of pastel spring flowers. The soft music kept the whispers to a minimum as Noah, Jerry, and the minister shifted their feet and waited.

The groom stood, handsome in his black tux, nervous, eyes darting to the archway, wondering why his soon-to-be mother-in-law had not made her appearance there. The room was beginning to feel too warm; his collar felt too tight. A lump formed in his throat as his eyes rested on the bouquet of white roses on the empty chair where his mother would have been seated. He wished that she was there, smiling at him, making him feel calm.

On the string quartet's third piece, a smiling Alison appeared and glided to her place. She was radiant in a shimmering lavender crepe that clung to her hourglass figure. Her dark hair, still damp from the impromptu shower, was simply finger-combed and sprayed, and her favorite scent, Lily of the Valley, filled the room. She winked at Noah, and he sighed with relief and began to relax.

Lee-Ann followed, smiling and nodding to each in the small gathering, loving her moment in the spotlight. The pale pink chiffon floated around her shapely calves as she gracefully took her place in front of a bank of ferns.

As the quartet struck up The Wedding March, Ginny paused at the top of the stairs and smiled down at John as he waited to escort her to the altar. In the light from the stained glass window, she appeared ethereal as she floated down the steps and took his arm.

"You are so beautiful," he whispered, in awe of this lovely creature, this young woman whom he had come to love so dearly. She smiled up at him, so obviously his daughter with her curly red hair and green eyes. The elegant dress, its threads of pink and silver glittering in the candlelight, skimmed over her slender frame. The simple veil fell from her upswept curls to the hem of the dress.

He proudly led her to the archway and to the altar, than took a chair behind Alison. Ginny had asked that the phrase 'Who gives this woman?' be omitted to avoid any undue attention to her parents' situation. As for herself, she was happy for everyone to know that John was her father.

She never took her eyes from Noah's as their minister, in his deep melodious voice, began the ceremony. Noah was so entranced with his beautiful bride that he stuttered his way through the vows, making Ginny giggle and the small audience smile in sympathy. Ginny repeated her vows clearly with tears of joy in her eyes. As they were pronounced man and wife, Noah swept her into a long kiss, and the guests stood and applauded.

Charles kept the camera rolling throughout the ceremony and followed them into the hall where they greeted their guests, then to the dining room where they posed for more pictures. Alison directed their friends to the buffet, and soon they were mingling and enjoying the repast Grace and Gloria served. Chairs were turned into groupings, and some of the guests went to the porch where three tables were set up.

"What a lovely yard," Ginny's principal remarked to Alison. "The flowers are so pretty; Ginny talks about her garden a lot. But what is that unusual red stuff growing in the grass over there." He pointed at the residue from Grover's bath.

Alison laughed. "It's the remains of several cans of tomatoes. Ginny's dog…" she began, nodding at a miserable Grover who lay with his head on his paws at the end of his tether. Soon the tale of Grover and the skunk got around and brought chuckles and other stories of wedding mishaps.

After all the pictures were taken, Ginny and Noah filled their plates along with Jerry, the best man, and Lee-Ann.

"Well, Cuz, you made it through. Ah'm just glad it wasn't you who went out after that mutt. A smelly bride would have been a real disaster," Lee-Ann said as she popped a miniature quiche into her mouth.

"I resent Grover being called a mutt. He's very intelligent. I just forgot to warn him about skunks, that's all. Everything else went beautifully, didn't it?" Ginny beamed at Noah.

He leaned over for a kiss. "It was perfect. Remind me later to tell you how utterly beautiful you are. Oh, and you looked good yourself, Lee-Ann."

"Ah think y'all had better hurry and get on with the honeymoon," she teased as she rose. "Ah haven't talked much with my parents today, hardly had time to see them." She kissed Ginny on the cheek and whispered. "Ah am so ready to go home to mah husband."

"Is it anywhere near time to leave?" Noah murmured anxiously in her ear.

"Another hour, darling, and we're on our way."

After mingling and talking for a while longer, they slipped upstairs to change into comfortable clothes for the trip. The small group gathered on the front lawn to see them off. Somehow, Jerry found time to decorate the car with the usual tissue and shaving crème, and it sat conspicuously ready for their departure. Running through the hail of birdseed, they paused to hug and kiss Alison, John, and Grace. Then, waving to all, they drove away, crepe paper streamers flying and cans dragging.

When the last guest left, Grace flopped down on the sofa. "Whew! I'm glad that's over. But wasn't it nice?"

"Thanks to all of you. Gloria, Charles, thanks. Lee-Ann, honey, you were great." Alison sat by Grace and put her arm around the older woman. "And you, my dear—we couldn't have done it without you."

"Well, we'd better not get too comfortable, there's a lot to clean up." Wearily, they all pitched in, the women dealing with food and dishes, the men re-arranging the furniture and vacuuming. By nine o'clock, all was back to normal.

Since she and John would be alone in the house, Alison decided she should spend the night with Grace, just in case the neighbors might wonder. John walked her over and held her for a long time at the back door.

"Ginny was so happy, wasn't she? She was just radiant."

"Yes, she was," Alison said, burying her face in his neck, suddenly aware that, if he weren't holding her up, she would collapse with fatigue.

"What time tomorrow?" he asked.

"I can be ready by ten."

"And it's all set up with Grace?"

"She knows the plan."

Chapter 35

The sun slipped down behind the mountain as they walked hand in hand to the German restaurant, John in his best suit, and Alison in her mother-of-the-bride dress. She paused before they entered to smell the petunias that bloomed in huge barrels just outside the quaint Dutch door.

"Just look at all these colors. I didn't know they came in so many shades. So lovely. I want one of every color on my porch."

John wished for a camera at that moment to catch the look of joy in her dark eyes, the shine of her hair curling softly around her ears, the way the lavender dress clung to her body. He would stamp that vision in his mind forever.

She laughed. "You're starving, and I'm smelling flowers. Sorry, darling." She patted his cheek as they stepped into the alpine décor of the place. A blond lady in braids and peasant attire escorted them to a table by the window overlooking the valley. They gave their drink orders and gazed into the growing twilight. Here and there, lights came on in the houses that were sprinkled among the fields and woods, bathed in a faint pink haze from the sunset.

"Beautiful," she said with a sigh.

"Yes, you are, especially in that dress. Or have I told you that before?"

"Not for the last ten minutes, but I forget easily. You'll have to tell me more often." She squeezed his hand across the table. "I'm so happy, John. I never thought I could be so happy."

"I feel like a giddy kid," he said, leaning in toward her. "I feel like jumping up and down, yelling, telling everyone I see that this wonderful, gorgeous woman loves me. Me!"

The waitress stood patiently until they finally glanced up, embarrassed, and apologized for ignoring her. She left their hot tea and took their order, smiling broadly at the antics of the newlyweds.

John took both of her hand in his. "I'll never forget that you wanted to come here to Laurel Springs, of all the places we could have gone. I never expected you to do that."

"I love it here. When Ginny was hurt, I came to like this town, and I've always loved the mountains, especially in the spring and in the fall. This is your home. So that's where I want to be."

"This is a beautiful place. I've always been glad that we moved here years ago. And with Calley buried here, I would have a difficult time living anywhere else, although I'd follow you anywhere."

She leaned forward and rubbed the fine red hair on his forearm. "Will you take me to her grave later on?"

With a lump in his throat, he nodded and whispered, "I love you."

Their sauerbraten was served, and they dug into the steaming dish. But neither could eat half of what was on their plates. Food was not what they had on their minds at the moment.

It was completely dark when they left the restaurant, and Alison asked to be driven through the curving streets of the town. The shops were still open, and tourists meandered in and out. The old hotel at the top of the mountain was aglow as they drove around it and back down to the residential area and Calley's Cottage. They pulled around to the garage in back and climbed the steps of the back porch. Alison started in.

"Oh, no," he said softly as he bent to pick her up. "I've waited a long time to carry you over the threshold, Mrs. Fredericks. Welcome home."

"Oh, John, I'm too heavy…your surgery…" He silenced her with a kiss that lasted long after he put her down, leaving them both weak. Taking her hand, he led her to the bedroom where he turned on the light.

She gasped. He had bouquets of pink roses on the bedside table, yellow ones on the chest, and a variegated red on the side table by the rocker. The aroma was intoxicating. "Oh, this is heavenly. When did you have a chance to order roses?"

"My…OUR neighbor, Mrs. Banks. She's a real romantic and was overjoyed to take care of it for me. We'll walk over and thank her tomorrow if you'd like." He nervously began to turn down the spread on the old antique bed, talking as he tossed the decorative pillows on the chair. "Ginny is supposed to call you on your cell, isn't she?"

"She said she would phone after dinner tonight. I'm surprised that she hasn't called already."

"You're sure she won't be upset with us for not telling her that we were getting married?"

"Maybe surprised but not upset. I didn't want to steal any attention from her wedding day, one of the most important days of her life. She'll understand that we didn't want to wait nor make a big production out of our wedding. I know she'll be very happy for us, especially when I tell her I've left my job and plan to move here and help you run this bed and breakfast again. She loves this place so much. Most of all, she'll be delighted to have her parents together. She's come to love you, John. She's so happy having you in her life."

"Do you think she might…you know…call me 'Dad' someday?" he asked, with a touch of sadness in his voice.

Alison came quickly into his arms and held him close, slowly kissing his lips, his face. "I know she will, my love."

Ginny slid her phone back into her purse.

"That's odd. I wonder where Mom is. Her cell phone is turned off, and she's not at our house or her apartment."

"Did you call Grace?"

"No. I'll just wait and call again tomorrow. I'm sure someone would have let us know if anything was wrong." She slipped her arm around Noah's waist as they walked barefoot along the beach.

"She's probably out with friends and forgot to turn on her phone."

"Do you think Mom and John are getting any closer? It seems to me they are. Having my father walk me down the aisle was like a dream come true. My life is complete now, almost like I found a piece of myself that was lost. And I have you to thank for finding him." She raised her face for his kiss. "I'm so happy, Noah. I just wish Mom could be this happy someday."

"Maybe she will, honey. Maybe she will." He pulled her to a stop. "Just look at that moon over the ocean. Is that not a beautiful sight?"

"It's perfect. Big moon, waves lapping at the shore, and my husband's arms around me. Talk about heaven on earth."

They stood for a long time, locked in each other's arms. Then slowly they walked down the beach toward their hotel holding hands, the ocean breeze blowing their hair and carrying their laughter out to sea.

To order additional copies of

Calley's Cottage

Have your credit card ready and call:

1-877-421-READ (7323)

or please visit our web site at
www.pleasantword.com

Also available at:
www.amazon.com
and
www.barnesandnoble.com

Printed in the United States
46485LVS00001B/13-36

9 781414 105611